LOVE CASTS OUT FEAR

Barbara Cartland

SEVERN HOUSE PUBLISHERS

This hard cover edition first published in the U.S.A. 1988 by
SEVERN HOUSE PUBLISHERS INC.
First World edition published in Great Britain 1986 by
SEVERN HOUSE PUBLISHERS LTD. of
40–42 William IV Street, London WC2N 4DF.

Reprinted 1988

British Library Cataloguing in Publication Data
Cartland, Barbara
Love casts out fear.
I. Title
823′.912[F]   PR6005.A765
ISBN 0 7278 1320 X

Printed and bound in Great Britain

ABOUT THE AUTHOR

Barbara Cartland, the world's most famous romantic novelist, who is also an historian, playwright, lecturer, political speaker and television personality, has now written over 400 books and sold over 390 million books over the world.

She has also had many historical works published and has written four autobiographies as well as the biographies of her mother and that of her brother, Ronald Cartland, who was the first Member of Parliament to be killed in the last war. This book has a preface by Sir Winston Churchill and has just been republished with an introduction by Sir Arthur Bryant.

Love at the Helm, a novel written with the help and inspiration of the late Earl Mountbatten of Burma, Uncle to His Royal Highness Prince Philip, is being sold for the Mountbatten Memorial Trust.

Miss Cartland in 1978 sang an *Album of Love Songs* with the Royal Philharmonic Orchestra.

In 1976 by writing twenty-one books, she broke the world record and has continued for the following eight years with twenty-four, twenty, twenty-three, twenty-four, twenty-four, twenty-five, twenty-two and twenty-six. In the *Guinness Book of Records* she is listed as the world's top-selling author.

In private life Barbara Cartland, who is a Dame of

Grace of the Order of St. John of Jerusalem, Chairman of the St. John Council in Hertfordshire and Deputy President of the St. John Ambulance Brigade, has fought for better conditions and salaries for Midwives and Nurses.

She has championed the cause for old people, had the law altered regarding gypsies and founded the first Romany Gypsy camp in the world.

Barbara Cartland is deeply interested in Vitamin therapy, and is President of the National Association for Health.

Her designs *Decorating with Love* are being sold all over the U.S.A. and the National Home Fashions League made her, in 1981, "Woman of Achievement".

Barbara Cartland's book *Getting Older, Growing Younger*, and her cookery book *The Romance of Food* have been published in Great Britain, the U.S.A., and in other parts of the world.

She has also written a Children's Pop-Up Book entitled *Princess to the Rescue*.

In 1984, she received at Kennedy Airport, America's Bishop Wright Air Industry Award for her contribution to the development of aviation when in 1931 she and two R.A.F. officers thought of, and carried, the first aeroplane-towed glider air-mail.

OTHER BOOKS BY
BARBARA CARTLAND

Romantic Novels, over 370, the most recently published being:

The Peril and the Prince
Alone and Afraid
Temptation for a Teacher
The Devilish Deception
In Paradise
Love is a Gamble
A Victory for Love
Look With Love
Never Forget Love
Safe at Last
Royal Punishment

Helga in Hiding
Haunted
Crowned With Love
Escape
The Devil Defeated
The Secret of the Mosque
A Dream in Spain
The Love Trap
Listening to Love
The Golden Cage

The Dream and the Glory (in aid of the St. John Ambulance Brigade)

Autobiographical and Biographical:

The Isthmus Years 1919–1939
The Years of Opportunity 1939–1945
I Search for Rainbows 1945–1976
We Danced All Night 1919–1929
Ronald Cartland (With a Foreword by Sir Winston Churchill)
Polly – My Wonderful Mother
I Seek the Miraculous

Historical:

Bewitching Women
The Outrageous Queen (The Story of Queen Christina of Sweden)
The Scandalous Life of King Carol
The Private Life of Charles II
The Private Life of Elizabeth, Empress of Austria

Josephine, Empress of France
Diane de Poitiers
Metternich – the Passionate Diplomat

Sociology:

You in the Home	Etiquette
The Fascinating Forties	The Many Facets of Love
Marriage for Moderns	Sex and the Teenager
Be Vivid, Be Vital	The Book of Charm
Love, Life and Sex	Living Together
Vitamins for Vitality	The Youth Secret
Husbands and Wives	The Magic of Honey
Men are Wonderful	The Book of Beauty and Health

Keep Young and Beautiful by Barbara Cartland and Elinor Glynn
Etiquette for Love and Romance
Barbara Cartland's Book of Health

Cookery:

Barbara Cartland's Health Food Cookery Book
Food for Love
Magic of Honey Cookbook
Recipes for Lovers
The Romance of Food

Editor of:

The Common Problem by Ronald Cartland (With a Preface by
    the Rt. Hon. the Earl of Selborne, P.C.)
Barbara Cartland's Library of Love
Barbara Cartland's Library of Ancient Wisdom
"Written with Love" Passionate love letters selected by Barbara
    Cartland

Drama:

Blood Money
French Dressing

Philosophy:

Touch the Stars

Radio Operetta:

The Rose and the Violet (Music by Mark Lubbock) performed in 1942.

Radio Plays:

The Caged Bird: An episode in the Life of Elizabeth Empress of Austria. Performed in 1957.

General:

Barbara Cartland's Book of Useless Information, With a Foreword by The Earl Mountbatten of Burma
(In aid of the United World Colleges)
Love and Lovers (Picture Book)
The Light of Love (Prayer Book)
Barbara Cartland's Scrapbook
(In aid of the Royal Photographic Museum)
Romantic Royal Marriages
Barbara Cartland's Book of Celebrities
Getting Older, Growing Younger

Verse:

Lines on Life and Love

Music:

An Album of Love Songs sung with the Royal Philharmonic Orchestra

Film:

The Flame is Love

Cartoons:

Barbara Cartland Romances (Book of Cartoons) has recently been published in the U.S.A. and Great Britain and in other parts of the world.

Children's Pop-Up Book
Princess to the Rescue

LOVE CASTS OUT FEAR

AUTHOR'S NOTE

On the 28th July, 1816, the Duke of Wellington gave his great Ball in his mansion in the Champs Elysées, in honour of the Royal Princes.

Strangely, the Princes left early, and in the small hours of the morning part of the basement was found to be on fire.

Gunpowder shavings and cartridges had been pushed through the bars of an area window, shattering the bars and setting the floorboards alight. Footmen quickly extinguished the flames and the Duke made light of the whole incident, yet many people alleged it was a Royalist crime.

The Army of Occupation of one hundred and fifty thousand British soldiers in France which was garrisoned at Cambrai after Napoleon Bonaparte's defeat at the Battle of Waterloo, ended in 1818.

Britain had only one hero, the Duke of Wellington. His conduct as a soldier, administrator and financier over the last three years, gave him a position in Europe no Englishman had ever achieved before. He returned home with the batons of six foreign countries in his knapsack.

The affection the Duke had for the three beautiful American Caton girls, and the way he tried to marry two of them to his titled *Aides-de-Camp* is factual.

CHAPTER ONE
1816

"It's no use, Miss Alecia, you can't make bricks without straw, and I can't cook food without having the money to buy it!"

"I know, Bessie," Alecia replied, "but Papa is very worried at the moment, and I do not wish to trouble him."

"That's all very well, Miss, but we can't go on as we are. And if you asks me, what your father needs is a piece of good beef-steak or a fat chicken or two."

Alecia sighed because she knew that Bessie, who had been looking after them for fifteen years, was speaking the truth.

But her father's last book had sold so few copies that it had left them almost penniless, and the one he was writing now would not be ready for at least another three or four months.

"What am I to do?" she asked herself, and wished, as she had a thousand times before, that the Earl of Langhaven had not died.

He had been her uncle, her mother's brother, and because he was fond of his sister he had been unfailingly kind to them.

When Lady Sophie insisted on marrying Troilus Stambrook her brother had been the only member of her family who did not rage at her and, as soon as he

1

inherited his father's title, he had given her and her erudite husband practical help.

Lady Sophie had fallen in love with the extremely handsome Troilus Stambrook when he came to tutor her brother before he went up to Oxford hoping, if not to get a degree, at least not to be sent down for total incompetence.

Troilus Stambrook was bowled over by the beauty of his employer's daughter, who had already captivated London Society with her charm and her elegance.

Although Lady Sophie had a number of suitors, one of them in her father's estimation extremely suitable and to whom he was prepared to give his unqualified blessing as a Son-in-law, she found that once she had met Troilus Stambrook no other man existed in the whole world.

A raging battle then ensued which continued until everybody was exhausted, and which ended, because she was so deeply in love and was prepared to fight the whole world if necessary, in Lady Sophie getting her own way.

So Lady Sophie, the toast of St. James's, married an obscure, unknown writer whose only qualification was that he was a Gentleman by birth, and because he was so clever he had won a scholarship to Eton and another to Oxford.

"You will rue the day you did anything so stupid!" the old Earl said to his daughter as they drove side by side to the small Church in the village where she was to be married.

But he was wrong, for Lady Sophie was blissfully happy, until the day she died.

The only problem had been that she and her husband had so little money, and after their daughter Alecia was born it was extremely difficult to make ends meet, and she was too proud to keep asking her father for help.

When her brother inherited, everything was different.

First of all, because he loved his sister, he gave her and her husband a little Manor house on the estate where they lived rent free, and saw they were supplied with food from his farms and gardens.

There were peaches and grapes from the hot-houses, any vegetables they required from the kitchen-gardens, and every week butter, cream and eggs came to the Manor from the Home Farm.

There were also chickens, ducks, fat pigeons and, in the Spring, legs of lamb which was one of the Earl's specialities.

This made life very much easier and Troilus Stambrook could concentrate on his writing and not feel humiliated by the knowledge that he was depriving the wife he adored of the luxuries which had been hers ever since she was born.

Then, just after Lady Sophie died in the bitter winter of 1814, her brother the Earl of Langhaven had a riding accident.

It left him crippled, and after enduring agonising pain for two months he, too, died.

It was then, when the new Earl took over Lang Hill and the estate, that everything had changed again for Alecia and her father.

The third Earl had had no son to continue his generosity because he, like his sister Sophie, had only one daughter whose name was Charis.

The two girls had been born within three weeks of one another, Alecia being the elder. They had played together and as soon as they were old enough shared a Governess.

It was only to be expected that Alecia should be the cleverer of the two, because her father always talked to her as if she was his equal and gave her lessons that were far beyond the range of any Governess.

But Charis shared them with her and, although she did not learn half as much as her cousin, they were very happy together.

Alecia's life was a joy from the moment she woke up in the morning to the time she went to bed at night.

She loved the lessons she had with her father, enjoyed those which took place up at the 'Big House' in the large, airy School-room.

But most of all, she adored riding with Charis on the well-bred, well-trained horses that belonged to her uncle.

When he died she could hardly believe that everything she knew and loved had come to an end.

It had been agonising to lose her mother, but she also lost Charis who, of course, had had to leave her home and the horses that were so much a part of her life.

She felt as if suddenly she had been swept from the warmth of a fire into the frightening ice-cold of a world outside that she had never known before.

When the new Earl took over, all the luxuries which Alecia had taken for granted ceased abruptly.

The new and fourth Earl was a very distant cousin, a rather raffish young man, unmarried, who enjoyed London and had no intention of burying himself in the country.

He was quite prepared to come down occasionally to his newly-acquired country seat, bringing with him large house-parties of beautiful women and men like himself who wanted to ride in the daytime and gamble through the night staking a fortune on the turn of a card.

To Alecia the tales that reached her of what the village called 'the goings on' up at Lang Hill seemed incredible.

She could hardly believe they were taking place in what had always been to her a second home.

"If your dear mother knew what was a-happening!" Bessie said over and over again, "she'd turn over in her grave, that she would!"

"Well, what is happening?" Alecia asked.

"Nothing as is fit for your ears, Miss Alecia!" Bessie replied, "but there's ladies rouged, powdered, and covered in furs and jewels, and gentlemen drinking enough claret to drown themselves, besides staking great piles of gold sovereigns which is disgraceful, if you ask me, seein' how much suffering there is 'cos of the war."

Alecia agreed with her because she was deeply perturbed by the treatment suffered by the men who had been demobilised from the Services now that the war with Napoleon was ended.

Without a pension, without any recompense for the years in which they had fought so bravely, most of them were unable to find work.

One thing that was obvious to Alecia was that the fourth Earl of Langhaven was not interested in his cousin who lived at the Manor House, nor for that matter in the concerns of any of the other people on his estate.

He did not visit the farmers which gave them offence, and he spoke only to the game-keepers about the prospects of the shooting in the Autumn.

After every visit, when he could be seen riding in the distance, he and his party would drive back to London in their Phaetons and travelling-chariots without having exchanged a word with those who lived in the shadow of Lang Hall.

"How can he behave so badly, Papa?" Alecia asked indignantly when after the Earl's third visit he had still made no effort to come in contact with anybody on the estate.

"I am afraid it is modern manners, my dear," Troilus Stambrook replied, "but as your cousin is *persona grata* with the Prince Regent, I imagine he does not think he should waste his time on people like us!"

"I will go to see him," Alecia decided to herself, "then perhaps I can persuade him to go on being kind to us as Uncle Lionel used to be."

She thought of walking up to the Big House and asking to see the Earl.

But it was not only her shyness which prevented her from doing so, but also her pride which would not allow her to humiliate herself by begging.

At the same time she had to face the fact that things were growing more and more desperate, and money was shorter and shorter.

Her mother's allowance, which was never a very large one, had stopped when she died, and it was only then that Alecia realised how little her father earned by his writing.

His books were clever, but far too erudite for the general public and, while they were appreciated by scholars, Dons and University Librarians, the amount they brought in was so infinitesimal that Alecia understood that it was with reluctance that the publishers agreed to take another of his books.

'I shall have to do something,' she thought now as she walked from the kitchen.

She left Bessie muttering that luncheon would consist of a few vegetables and little else unless the hens in the garden would lay another egg, which was extremely unlikely as they had had two for breakfast.

"I shall have to do something!" Alecia repeated.

She could not imagine what she could do, and there was nothing left in the house that they could sell.

She wept bitterly when her father disposed of a few pieces of jewellery which had belonged to her mother.

She had also cried when the china figures, mostly of Dresden, which her mother had collected over the years, many which she had brought with her when she married, had been sold for a few pounds.

Now there was nothing left except for the furniture that was worn and badly in need of being recovered, and a portrait of her mother which hung in her father's Study.

It had been painted when she first went to London and had become a social success overnight.

'We cannot sell that,' Alecia thought. 'If that was taken away it would break Papa's heart.'

She knew that her father thought of the portrait as his inspiration, and when he was alone he would look up at the picture and talk to his wife as if she was still alive.

It was only by burying himself in his writing that her father was able to forget the agony of his loss, and go on living without a wife.

"What can I do? What can I do?" Alecia asked herself again and again.

Finally, she decided to swallow her pride and was just about to walk up to the Hall when she was surprised to hear a carriage draw up outside the front door, and wondered who it could be.

She saw so few people these days, and anyway, as it was morning, it was an unusual time for anyone to call.

There came a loud rat-tat and it never crossed Alecia's mind that she should wait for Bessie to open the door, but hurried to do so herself.

Then she stood transfixed to see the elegant travelling-carriage which stood outside and the person who was stepping out of it.

Suddenly she gave a cry of delight that seemed to echo out into the spring sunshine.

"Charis! Can it really be you?"

Lady Charis Langley ran towards her cousin and flung her arms around her.

"Alecia, dearest! I am so thrilled to see you!"

The cousins kissed each other, then with their arms entwined they walked through the hall and into the Drawing-Room.

"How could I have guessed .. how could I have imagined that you would suddenly turn up like this?" Alecia was saying. "Oh, Charis, I have missed you and you have not written to me for nearly two months."

"I know, dearest, and you must forgive me," Charis replied, "and now I have so much to tell you, I hardly know where to begin!"

Lady Charis's mother had died very tragically when she was only a little girl, and after her father's death she had gone to London to live with an Aunt, the Duchess of Hampden, who had, as soon as she was out of mourning, presented her at Buckingham Palace.

Before this there had been, however, innumerable small dinner-parties and entertainments which Charis had never experienced before, but which obviously delighted her.

At first after leaving the country she had written to

Alecia almost every day, telling her how much she missed her and relating everything that was happening in London.

When the letters became less frequent, Alecia realised that Charis was busy with new friends and, although she was sure she still loved her, there was a great deal to occupy her days.

Then, since the beginning of the year, Charis's letters had grown even fewer, and when she did write it was obvious that she did not have time to write down for Alecia everything she was doing.

However, now she was here and Alecia could only gasp at the difference in her appearance from when she had seen her last.

Then she had been miserable and unhappy over the death of her father, and frightened of going away from the only home she had ever known.

She had left in a flood of tears, looking in her black gown and bonnet very unlike the laughing lovely girl with whom Alecia had shared her life for eighteen years.

Now as she looked at her cousin she realised she was dressed in the very latest fashion, very different from anything she had ever seen before, and she had a new beauty that seemed all together breath-taking.

Charis took off her high-crowned bonnet which was trimmed with small ostrich feathers and threw it on a chair.

Then she drew Alecia down beside her on the sofa and said:

"You look just the same! Have you missed me?"

"Terribly!" Alecia replied. "Nothing has been the same since you left, and everything is strange and rather horrible since the new Earl took your father's place."

"I am not surprised," Charis said. "I never did like Cousin Gerald, and when I see him in London he is always with some actress or Cyprian, so that it is impossible for me to speak to him."

Alecia's eyes widened.

"Do you think those are the women he brings here?"

"I would not be surprised," Charis answered, "although he spends quite a lot of his time with the Prince Regent."

It passed through Alecia's mind that the Prince Regent's reputation had shocked most of the older people in the village, but before she could say anything Charis said:

"But I did not come here to talk about Cousin Gerald. It is about myself, and oh, Alecia, you have to help me!"

"Of course, dearest, I will do anything you want, although it is very difficult for me to think how I could possibly help you."

As she spoke she was admiring not only Charis's elegant, fashionable gown, which looked extremely expensive, but also the string of perfect pearls round her neck.

She wore too a gold bracelet set with small diamonds on her wrist, and a very valuable diamond ring on the third finger of her right hand, which seemed somehow a little ostentatious for a young girl.

Then she realised that Charis, with whom she had been so familiar that she had always believed she could read her thoughts, was looking worried.

Because she was aware perceptively that something was wrong she said quickly:

"What is it, Charis? Tell me how I can help you."

Charis looked down at the diamond ring on her right hand before she said:

"I am engaged to be married!"

Alecia gave a little cry.

"Oh, Charis. Why did you not tell me? How exciting! And of course, you will be very happy!"

"Very, very happy!" Charis agreed. "I am so lucky, Alecia, and Harry says he is the luckiest man in the whole world! But just at the moment there are difficulties."

"First of all," Alecia said, "who is Harry?"

"He is the Viscount Turnbury, son of the Earl of Scarcliffe," Charis replied proudly.

Alecia did not speak, she just listened as Charis went on:

"He is so handsome, so amusing, and to me the most wonderful man in the whole world!"

She smiled before she said:

"I love him, Alecia, in exactly the same way that Aunt Sophie loved your father, and if he had not a penny and was of no significance whatsoever I would be quite ready to run away with him."

"I have always hoped and prayed that you would love somebody like that," Alecia said, "but what is the difficulty?"

"That is what I have come to tell you."

Charis drew in a deep breath before she began:

"We knew as soon as we met each other that we were in love, and when Harry asked me to marry him, I wanted to tell everybody how happy we were. Then suddenly his mother died."

"I am sorry," Alecia murmured.

"We realised," Charis went on, "that we could hardly announce our engagement immediately after her death.

Then, while Harry was trying to think of a way by which we could avoid having to wait a whole year to be married, a terrible thing happened."

"What was it?" Alecia asked.

"I received a letter from my Guardian."

"From your Guardian?" Alecia echoed. "I did not know you had one!"

"Neither did I," Charis replied. "I seem to remember that Papa said something about it in the past, but I had forgotten all about it."

"Explain to me."

"When Papa went to Portugal with Wellington's Army right at the beginning of the war, I was twelve. One day shortly before they went into a battle, a Senior Officer commanding them suggested that they all make Wills leaving everything they possessed to the people they really wanted to have it."

"I can understand that was a sensible idea," Alecia said.

"I think Papa told me that some officers treated it very frivolously," Charis continued, "and left ridiculous things to people who would not want them, and treated the whole thing as a joke."

She gave a little sigh before she said:

"But Papa, for no reason I can understand, made a friend of his my Guardian, Lord Kiniston who is now a General."

"I suppose he thought he was a responsible person," Alecia said slowly. "Have you ever met him?"

"Of course not! As I say, I really did not know he existed until two days ago when I received a letter from France."

"From France?" Alecia questioned.

"He is at Cambrai with the Army of Occupation and I

gather from his letter that just as I did not know, or had forgotten about him, he had forgotten about me."

"Then why should he trouble you now?" Alecia enquired.

"I have no idea why," Charis replied, "but he has ordered me to join him in France, now! Immediately!"

Alecia stared at her.

"Do you really mean that? But how can he suggest such a thing?"

"He has not only suggested it, but he expects me to obey him," Charis replied, "which of course I have no intention of doing."

"Surely you can write to say it is not convenient?"

"Harry thinks that would be a mistake, and he thinks, too, that Lord Kiniston has some ulterior motive in asking me to go to Cambrai, where the English garrison is quartered. He is also afraid that if I do go Lord Kiniston will not let me come back."

"I cannot think of any reason why he should wish to detain you," Alecia said. "After all, if he is a proper sort of Guardian, surely he would be delighted for you to marry anyone so important as Viscount Turnbury?"

"He sounds as if he is such a stickler for etiquette, and all that sort of thing," Charis argued, "that he would not let us get married at once, which is what we are determined to do."

Alecia stared at her and Charis said:

"Harry has it all planned out and no one will know, except you, that we are going to be married almost immediately."

Alecia's eyes widened.

"How can you do that?"

"Quite easily," Charis smiled. "I am going to tell Aunt Emily that I am going away to stay with friends –

you will do as well as anybody – but actually Harry and I are going to be married very secretly, in some tiny country Church by Special Licence."

Her voice showed how excited she was as she went on:

"Then we are going to a house Harry owns in Suffolk, where no one will find us."

Alecia drew in her breath.

"I am sure you . . should not do . . this!"

"It is something I have every intention of doing!" Charis replied. "I love Harry and he loves me, more than anything else in the world. If I go away and leave him there will be other women who will try to get him into their clutches, and I might lose him."

"If he really loved you he would not look at anybody else."

Charis gave a little laugh.

"Dearest Alecia, men are men, and there is one particular woman, whom I absolutely hate, who has been trying to steal him from me for months. She is, I must admit, very beautiful and very sophisticated, and I am afraid he might be unable to resist her and would forget me."

"But surely that is impossible?" Alecia said. "No one could be as lovely as you, Charis!"

"Or as you!" Charis replied. "After all, we have always been very alike. Do you remember when we were children how we used to be taken for twins?"

Alecia laughed

"That was a long time ago, and I certainly do not look like your twin now."

"You would do if you were dressed like me, and did your hair in a fashionable way."

"What would be the point?" Alecia asked. "There is

14

no one here to see me except Papa who is absorbed in his writing and thinks only of Mama and how much he misses her, or old Bessie, who thinks of nothing but the food we have not got."

As she spoke she gave a little cry.

"Oh, Charis, are you staying for luncheon? Because if so, there is nothing to offer you."

"What do you mean – nothing to offer me?"

Alecia looked embarrassed.

"I am afraid it is the truth. You see, now that your father is no longer here, we do not have the delicious things from the gardens and farms as we used to, and Papa's last book made very little money."

Charis looked at her, then she said:

"I am ashamed of myself! How can I have been so selfish as not to realise that Papa's death would make such a difference to you? I am sorry, Alecia, I am really! You must forgive me."

"Dearest, it is not anything to do with you. It is just that things have been very difficult, and I do not know quite what to do about them."

"I will tell you the first thing you can do," Charis said. "You can tell the servants who brought me here to go out and buy some food for our luncheon."

She opened the pretty reticule she wore on her wrist and drawing out three golden sovereigns put them into Alecia's hand.

"I . . I cannot take . . this!" Alecia said weakly.

"Do not be so ridiculous!" Charis replied. "We shared everything in the past, and what I am going to ask you to do for me is worth a great deal more than that. Now go and tell Bessie to give the footman a list of what she wants, and to hurry up about it. Otherwise, we shall both be hungry!"

15

Alecia made a sound that was half a laugh and half a sob, then without saying any more she ran from the room.

She found Bessie in the kitchen and, as she expected, the coachman and footman who had brought Charis down from London were sitting at the kitchen table drinking cups of tea.

They both rose as she entered and she said good-morning to them before she drew Bessie out of the kitchen into the passage, and shut the door behind her.

"Now listen, Bessie," she said, "Lady Charis says she wants to pay for luncheon, and you are to order her coachman and footman to go into the village and buy anything you want. Here is a guinea, and I have some more, which we will save for Papa's food for the rest of the week."

Bessie stared at the golden sovereign as if she had never seen one before, then putting up her work-worn hand she took it saying:

"Glory be to God! And I was prayin' for a miracle!"

"Then your prayers are answered," Alecia said, "so hurry and tell them what you want."

Alecia went back into the Drawing-Room saying as she entered it:

"I am very, very grateful, Charis, dearest, but I feel it is somehow wrong to impose on you."

"You are not imposing on me," Charis replied, "and how can you have been so foolish as not to tell me of the situation you are in?"

Alecia did not answer, and Charis went on:

"All right, I have been very selfish in thinking only of myself, or rather of Harry, and that is why I am here now, and why you have to help me."

"You have still not told me what you want me to do," Alecia said.

"It is quite easy," Charis replied, "all you have to do is to go to France in my place, so that I can marry Harry as he wants me to do, and neither my tiresome old Guardian, nor anybody else, for that matter, will be able to stop us."

Alecia stared at Charis as if she thought she had taken leave of her senses.

- "I .. I do not know what you are .. saying," she stammered.

Charis drew in her breath.

"Both Harry and I think from my Guardian's letter that if I do not do as he wishes, he will be furious. He has given me minute instructions and I am to travel next Thursday, that is in three days' time, chaperoned by the wife of a Major in his Regiment, who is going out to join her husband. We are to be looked after by a competent Courier, chosen by him, and he has made everything he has arranged sound exactly like an Army exercise!"

"A.and you are suggesting that I should .. go, pretending to be you?"

Because Alecia was so astonished it was difficult for her to speak clearly.

"It will not be all that difficult," Charis replied. "If I refuse to do as Lord Kiniston asks, I am sure he is the type of man who will make a tremendous fuss and make it impossible for Harry and me to go away as we intend. Once we are married and have disappeared, there will be very little he can do about it."

"But .. why can you not write and tell him that is what you intend?"

"Do not be stupid, Alecia," Charis said. "He is the

kind of General who is used to having his orders obeyed to the letter and he likes everything to be exactly correct, conventional and punctilious."

Her tone of voice was sarcastic and scathing, and she went on:

"How could he possibly agree to my marrying somebody as important as Harry, when his mother has been dead for only a few weeks? Of course he will insist on our waiting for months and months, if not for the full year, and Harry agrees that we could not tolerate that, or being separated from each other, as we should be if I went to France."

"I do understand exactly what you are feeling," Alecia said, "but surely your Guardian will not believe that I am you?"

Charis laughed.

"Why not? We look very much alike, and in fact, he has never seen me, nor has the Major's wife with whom I am to travel, nor, I am certain, has anyone in Cambrai."

She made a little gesture with her hand before she went on:

"It is not as though you would be going to Paris, where there might be people who have seen me in London, although I rather doubt it. After all, my friends are not the slightest bit interested in the Army of Occupation, and the men who have come home are sick to death of fighting, and just want to enjoy themselves."

"I can understand that," Alecia said softly.

"All you have to do," Charis went on confidently, "is to dress like me, and you know me well enough to talk like me. Moreover, we have the same relatives, so that he can hardly trip you up on that score!"

"I .. I know I could not .. play a part like .. that," Alecia stammered.

Charis put out her hand and took hers.

"Dearest, you have to help me – there is no one else. If I lose Harry through leaving him I think I would want to die!"

Alecia was silent, then Charis said:

"Actually it was Harry who suggested before I came here that I might offer you a present for doing this for us. When he suggested it, I thought you might feel insulted, but now that I know what a mess you are in because Papa died, I am going to offer you £500 if you will go to France in my place, and stay there until it is safe for Harry and me to admit that we are married."

"£500?" Alecia gasped.

She was about to say it was something she could not accept and was, as Charis had envisaged, an insult.

Then she thought of her father, and knew that she could not deprive him of the food he needed and the freedom from worry.

As if she knew, without Alecia saying anything, that she had won her battle, Charis said:

"And now, dearest, we have a lot to do in a short time."

"What have we .. to do?" Alecia asked bewildered.

"We have to bring in the clothes I have brought for you from London, and plan exactly how you will pick up a great many more in the three days before you meet Mrs. Belton and set off across the Channel."

Alecia gave a little cry of protest.

"How can I do this, Charis? I shall let you down, I know I shall! And Lord Kiniston will be furiously angry if he finds out he is being deceived."

"Not if he does not find out too quickly!" Charis

said. "Then it will be too late for him to do anything about it, and he will not want to cause a scandal by exposing Harry as heartless for having married so soon after his mother's death, and putting me under suspicion of being obliged to marry in such haste!"

She saw by the expression on her cousin's face that Alecia did not understand what she was implying, and went on quickly:

"Just keep him calm and amused until I let you know what Harry and I are doing, and dearest, we shall both be so wildly and ecstatically happy that I know you will feel rewarded for your kindness to us."

Alecia felt as if her head was spinning, and that unexpectedly she had been swept into a whirlwind.

It was only when she and Charis had gone up to her bedroom and her cousin was arranging her hair in the same style as her own that Alecia said weakly:

"What . . am I to . . tell Papa?"

"Tell him I am taking you with me to London, which is something I should have done a long time ago, and will therefore not surprise him. In case you are worried about him while you are away, I suggest, if that nice Mrs. Milden is still living in 'The Towers' at the end of the village, you could ask her to keep an eye on him."

"Yes, she is still there," Alecia said, "but how could I suggest that she looks after Papa?"

"Easily!" Charis said. "If I know anything about it, she was always saying how wonderful he was, and how much she enjoyed reading his books, which is more than most people do! And now I come to think of it, as she is very well off, you have been very stupid not to make use of her before."

"I . . I never thought of it," Alecia said. "I suppose I thought of her more as Mama's friend than Papa's."

"If you ask me," Charis said with a worldly-wise air, "Mrs. Milden was much more anxious to be friends with your father than she ever was with your mother, but, of course, she was too careful to say so."

Thinking of Mrs. Milden, who was an attractive widow nearing forty, Alecia realised that every time she met her she had always suggested she and her father should come to luncheon or dinner with her. She had, too, seemed very disappointed when her father had refused.

"I am too busy with my book to be sociable," he had replied to every suggestion Alecia made.

Now she thought she should have insisted that Mrs. Milden, and perhaps other people in the neighbourhood, should visit him to give him something else to think about.

But because they had so little to offer by way of hospitality and after her mother's death her father was so distraught, she knew it was impossible for him to mix with other people.

She had just let things drift, and now she said:

"I will do as you suggest, Charis, I will go to see Mrs. Milden and ask her as a great favour, if she will look after Papa while I am away."

"I am sure she will be only too delighted," Charis replied, "and actually, I always liked her."

"I like her too," Alecia agreed, "and it was very stupid of me not to realise that if we had gone to dinner there as she suggested, we would at least have had one good meal!"

"That is something you will be able to have in the future," Charis said, "and if you do not see to it, I will!

After all, since Papa died I have a very large income of my own, although I am not allowed to touch the capital until I am twenty-one."

"Is Harry, the man you are going to marry, wealthy?" Alecia asked.

"He will be very rich when his father dies, but we have enough between us to do everything we want. Incidentally, what we both want most is a racing-stable!"

"A racing-stable?" Alecia repeated in surprise.

"That is another reason for our wanting to marry. I have not yet told you that my horrible old Guardian was reminded of my existence simply because I asked my Solicitors to let me have £20,000 with which to buy horses."

She made an exasperated little sound as she said:

"I see now it was silly of me, but Harry was planning the stable and saying we would manage it together as a joint concern. So while he was buying horses for it, I wanted to do the same."

"So that is why Lord Kiniston remembered about you!" Alecia exclaimed.

"Yes, and if only I had been sensible and realised something like that might happen, all this need never have arisen. At the same time, Harry says he always meant to run away with me for the simple reason he cannot possibly wait for months and months before it is conventional to announce our engagement, then wait again to be married."

Suddenly Charis threw her arms around Alecia's neck and kissed her.

"Now everything will be perfect," she said, "and thank you, thank you, dearest Alecia, for being so kind!"

"I .. I am frightened!" Alecia said in a very small voice.

"Nonsense!" Charis retorted. "It will be an adventure and it is high time you had one!"

CHAPTER TWO

Just before she reached the *Green Dragon* on the Dover Road, Alecia began to think she was crazy.

How could she have let Charis stampede her into doing anything so absurd as to impersonate her, not only to her Guardian, but also to a large number of people she would obviously meet at Cambrai.

She had an impulse to turn the smart travelling-chariot drawn by four horses which Charis had provided and insist that they take her home.

Yet she knew that because she loved her cousin she could not do anything so heartless or so cruel as to prevent her from marrying the man she loved.

In London Charis had talked and talked about how wonderful Harry Turnbury was, and when Alecia met him she could understand why she was so in love.

He was not only a very handsome, charming young man, but she knew perceptively that he was intelligent and reliable, qualities that would make him a good husband.

The way he thanked her for helping them and the way he looked at Charis told Alecia all she wanted to know. After that she ceased to protest at anything Charis suggested to her.

To her surprise, even though she knew it was under Harry's influence, Charis had everything mapped out in an efficient and sensible manner, which Alecia was sure she would have been unable to do a year ago.

Lord Kiniston in his letter, as Charis had already told her, had appointed a Mrs. Belton, the wife of a Major in his Regiment, to escort her on the journey to Cambrai.

It was Charis who saw the difficulty of a meeting in London where the servants would be aware that Alecia was not her.

"It has all been fixed, dearest," she said. "I have sent a note by one of the grooms to where Mrs. Belton is staying, apologising for not coming personally as I was so busy packing for the visit to my Guardian, and explaining that as I would be staying in the country to say goodbye to one of my relatives, I would meet her at the *Green Dragon*, which I know is a Posting House about three-quarters of the way to Dover."

As the *Green Dragon* was very much nearer to Alecia's home this made it an easy journey for her, especially with the superb horses which Charis had sent to convey her.

The moment they had arrived together in London Charis had started to provide Alecia with a new wardrobe that left her gasping.

Not only did she buy her a number of gowns that could be finished in the little time they had, but she also gave her dozens of her own things which not only fitted Alecia, but became her in the same way as they had made Charis the best-dressed débutante of the previous year.

"I am going to have everything new for my trousseau," she told Alecia, "and as I can afford it, why not?"

She put her arms around her cousin as she spoke and said:

"If you say 'No' to one single thing I give you, I shall be very hurt. I am really salving my conscience for not having remembered while I was having such a wonderful time that you were left behind in the country with no one to admire you."

"I was very happy, until Mama died," Alecia said, "and I was so delighted to hear of your success and how beautiful everybody thought you were."

"You are just as beautiful as I am," Charis replied, "and let us hope that the whole of the Army of Occupation realises it!"

Alecia laughed.

"One hundred and fifty thousand men!" she exclaimed. "That is really asking too much!"

"You can have every one of them," Charis said, "and the Duke of Wellington thrown in, as long as you leave me Harry."

There was a softness in her voice and a look in her eyes as she spoke that told Alecia how much she loved the Viscount.

She prayed fervently when she was alone at night that Charis would be really happy and never disillusioned.

She knew from the gossip she had heard even in the village of Little Langley how the Bucks and Beaux in London feted a beautiful woman one moment, and were bored with her the next.

Tales of how callous and heartless they were had often reached Alecia's ears, and she had been afraid that Charis, being so beautiful as well as having an important background and a rich father, would be married not for herself, but for her social position and her money.

But having seen Harry Turnbury she knew that, no less than Charis, he was wholeheartedly in love, and she told herself whatever they asked her to do and however difficult it might be, she must not fail them.

At the same time, she was well aware of how unsophisticated she was, and how ignorant of the Social World in which Charis shone so brightly.

When the horses turned in to the large yard of the *Green Dragon* her fingers were cold and she felt as if there were a hundred butterflies fluttering in her breast.

The one consolation was that her father would be well looked after, after she had left.

When she had gone to see Mrs. Milden she realised how stupid she had been since her mother's death in not encouraging her to continue to visit the house as she had always done, and to give her father a companionship which was different from that which she could give him.

Mrs. Milden was a quiet, pretty woman who at the same time had an excellent brain because she spent so much time reading, being too shy to make many social friends.

She had always loved Lady Sophie, who had loved her.

The way she greeted Alecia and listened to her attentively showed that she not only understood what the problem would be while she was away, but was willing to do anything that was required of her.

"Papa has been so unhappy since Mama died," Alecia said confidingly, "and although he often forgets I am there when he is writing his books, I know he hates having meals alone, and needs somebody to encourage him."

"What are you suggesting I do?" Mrs. Milden asked a little nervously.

"I was thinking that if you could have luncheon with Papa every day, and persuade him to have dinner with you, it would make things very much easier for Bessie, who finds it difficult cooking two meals a day, and the exercise of walking from the Manor House to yours would be very good for him."

"I understand, dear child, of course I do," Mrs. Milden said, "and I will try to persuade your father, but you must not be angry with me if he refuses."

"I do not think Papa will refuse you," Alecia said. "What he dislikes more than anything else is to be alone in the rooms in which everything reminds him of Mama and to know that she will not answer when he calls her."

She knew Mrs. Milden understood by the way in which she put her hand on hers and said:

"I will try! I will try, dear Alecia, to do everything I can to help your father, and of course you."

One thing which Alecia knew which made everything easier was that she would have enough money to buy food.

First, however, she had taken the carriage to the Market Town nearest to Little Langley and put the money in her father's name in the Bank.

"This is a pleasant surprise, Miss Stambrook," the Bank Manager said.

"I want to ask you a favour, Mr. Graham."

She knew the Bank Manager was listening as she went on:

"This money has been given to Papa by an admirer who would be very embarrassed if Papa found out about it."

Mr. Graham raised his eye-brows and Alecia explained:

"It is somebody who thinks his books are marvellous and who knows what very straitened circumstances we are in, but would not wish to hurt Papa's pride by asking him to accept such a large sum. I am therefore begging you not to send him any statement until I return home."

The Bank Manager nodded, thinking at the same time how lovely Alecia looked as she pleaded with him.

"I understand perfectly, Miss Stambrook," he said, "and I will personally see that no bank statements are sent until you advise us of your return, and any cheques your father writes will, of course, be honoured in the usual way."

"Thank you, Mr. Graham, thank you very much indeed," Alecia smiled.

When she got home she gave Bessie a large sum of money to pay every bill they owed in the neighbourhood.

Then she had enough money to provide her father with good, nourishing food for at least a month.

"With all this money lying about I'll be afraid of robbers!" Bessie exclaimed.

"Hide it somewhere," Alecia suggested. "You know as well as I do that no robbers would expect to find anything of any value in this house!"

Bessie laughed.

"You're right there, Miss Alecia, and it's a crying pity Lady Charis couldn't have been so generous before we had to dispose of your poor mother's jewels."

Because it made Alecia sad to think of it she did not answer, but merely said:

"Do not let Papa know that things are better than they have been for a long time. I doubt, in fact, if he will notice the difference anyway."

"He's not human, he's living in the clouds an' his feet never touches the ground!" Bessie said.

Then because she loved Alecia, she added:

"Now you take care of yourself, Miss Alecia, not that you don't deserve a good time with Her Ladyship. At the same time, you be careful o' them Rakes as you'll find in London. Many a decent girl has found her life ruined 'cos of them!"

Alecia had of course not told Bessie she was going abroad, and when the carriage arrived she was waiting in the hall so that the coachman would have no chance of saying they were not travelling to London, as Bessie and her father thought, but going to Dover.

Charis had told her that she had sent her own horses to the *Green Dragon* so that they would not be so long on the road as the posting-horses they would have had to employ were never of the best quality.

"I am afraid, dearest, you will have to be alone and unchaperoned for the first part of the journey," Charis had said, "but once you get to the *Green Dragon* you will find Mrs. Belton and the Courier whom Lord Kiniston has provided and, of course, a lady's-maid."

Alecia's eyes had widened.

"A lady's-maid!" she exclaimed. "But surely she will know I am not you?"

"I have thought it out carefully," Charis replied, "and I had to let Martha, who has been with me for years, into the secret that I am to marry Harry. She is delighted and has produced a relative whom she says is an excellent lady's-maid. She thinks that she will be travelling with me to France while Martha has a rest."

Alecia had laughed a little ruefully.

"It all gets more and more complicated," she said,

"and more and more frightening. You are quite sure the new maid will really think I am you?"

"Martha is as brilliant a liar as I am!" Charis said complacently.

She laughed before she added:

"Do you remember how when we were children I was always being punished for lying, while you were the goody-goody one, who never told a fib, and was always held up to me as a shining example?"

"I am sure that is not true," Alecia objected.

At the same time, she thought to herself that lies were unlucky, and she hoped she would not have to tell too many, even though she was acting a very large lie indeed in pretending to be Charis.

But from the moment she put on an extremely elegant blue travelling-gown with a cape edged with fur to wear on the voyage and the smartest bonnet she had ever possessed, she felt as if she had stepped into her new part, not only looking like Charis, but feeling like her.

She was well aware, however, that she had none of the self-confidence or the authority which Charis had acquired since she had been such a success in the Social World.

Alecia's pride forbade her to let herself appear as nervous as she felt and made her walk into the *Green Dragon* with her chin up.

The Landlord hurried forward to greet the occupant of such a smart travelling-carriage.

"I am Lady Charis Langley," Alecia managed to say, "and I think there is a Mrs. Belton waiting to see me."

"Yes, indeed, M'Lady," the Proprietor said, rubbing his hands together appreciatively. "If Your Ladyship'll come this way, I'll show you to th' Private Parlour."

He went ahead and Alecia followed him.

When he opened the door she saw to her relief that Mrs. Belton was quite a homely-looking woman with a pleasant smile and clothes that were in good taste, if not particularly expensive.

"Oh here you are, Lady Charis!" Mrs. Belton exclaimed. "I have been worrying in case anything should delay you and we would be too late arriving at Dover to catch the ship. Mr. Hunt tells me that it goes out on the tide."

Alecia looked enquiringly at the man who had risen at her entrance and realised, even before Mrs. Belton explained, that she was referring to the Courier whom Lord Kiniston had engaged to take them safely to Cambrai and who had come down with her from London.

Mr. Hunt obviously knew his place and having bowed to Alecia he went into the yard to supervise the changing of the horses and see that the coachmen had a quick meal before they proceeded on their way.

Food was also waiting for Alecia, and she thought that Lord Kiniston must be as efficient in his organisation as Charis was in hers.

Half-an-hour later she and Mrs. Belton were sitting comfortably behind fresh horses in the carriage, while the Courier and her lady's-maid, whom she had not yet seen, were following in another, also drawn by four horses, and carrying their baggage.

The road to Dover was good because it was frequently used by the Prince Regent, and they moved at a far quicker pace than Alecia expected, and quick enough to prevent Mrs. Belton from worrying whether they would miss the ship.

They had not driven far before Alecia found that

Mrs. Belton was an inveterate gossip and an unceasing talker.

She chatted away about her time in London, how much she was looking forward to seeing her husband again, and how boring he, like most of his officers, was finding his job with the Army of Occupation, because they had so little to do.

"War is one thing, Lady Charis, but peace is another," Mrs. Belton said, "and one cannot really blame a man for preferring the excitement of war."

"I think war is terrifying," Alecia replied.

"Well, you must not say so to your Guardian," Mrs. Belton laughed, "considering the success war has brought him."

"Success?" Alecia queried.

She realised how little she knew about Lord Kiniston and that perhaps this was a good opportunity to learn something about him.

"You must be aware, Lady Charis, that Lord Kiniston is one of the most brilliant soldiers we have ever had in the British Army, with the exception of course, of His Grace."

"No, I did not know," Alecia murmured.

"Well, to begin with, he is the youngest General . ."

"The *youngest*?" Alecia interrupted. "I thought he would be quite old."

Mrs. Belton laughed.

"Oh, no, dear, you have got it all wrong. He cannot yet be more than thirty-three, and he was made a General after a battle in which his Commanding Officer was killed and he took over and used such outstandingly brilliant tactics that the Frenchies all ran away and our losses were infinitesimal."

"Only thirty-three!" Alecia murmured beneath her breath.

"Yes, that is all," Mrs. Belton said, "but you will find him rather awe-inspiring. They say he has modelled himself on His Grace, but quite frankly I find the Duke easier to talk to, and in a way far more human than Lord Kiniston."

"In what way?" Alecia enquired.

"Well, he has a manner . ." Mrs. Belton said as if she was feeling for words, "a sort of . . looking through you . . I cannot explain it . . but it is as if he suspects you have something hidden beneath the surface, which is more interesting than what he can see at a casual glance."

She made a gesture with her gloved hands as she said:

"Oh, I cannot explain it . . I never was good at analysing people, but that is what Lord Kiniston does, from all I hear, and the Duke relies on him, knowing that if a man is hiding a secret, Lord Kiniston will be aware of it."

Alecia drew in her breath.

This sounded very alarming and she wondered what would happen if the moment she arrived Lord Kiniston knew that she was hiding a secret, and demanded an explanation.

Then she told herself there was no reason for him to suspect for one moment that she was not everything she pretended to be.

Mrs. Belton was still talking.

"Of course," she said, "you will understand that being so young and so handsome and of course so very, very rich, women find your Guardian irresistible."

"Women?" Alecia faltered. "I did not .. think there would be many at Cambrai."

She had envisaged in her own mind that a garrison town would be crowded with soldiers all in uniform, while the officers like Lord Kiniston would be extremely preoccupied with keeping order and of course drilling the troops.

Mrs. Belton was laughing again.

"I can see you are in for a surprise, Lady Charis!" she said. "You have been thinking, as I did myself, that life at Cambrai means the austerity and discomfort of a barracks, but I can promise you that life there is better than that!"

She went on to explain that the Duke of Wellington had taken a Château at Mont-Saint-Martin, which was about twelve miles from his Headquarters in Cambrai.

"Actually he set an example," Mrs. Belton said, "for Lord Kiniston immediately found another Château, almost as large as the Duke's, and most beautifully furnished. Whenever I have been there, I always envy his guests."

"I .. do not understand," Alecia managed to say. "I did not know there would be much entertainment at Cambrai, although I knew the Duke had a house in Paris."

She had learnt all this from Charis, but because her cousin had been certain she would not be called upon to go to Paris, she had not paid much attention.

It had never struck her that there would be any sort of society in a garrison town.

"Well, I can see you are in for a surprise!" Mrs. Belton said again, "and because you are attractive, my dear, I think Lady Lillian Somerset will also be surprised!"

"Who is Lady Lillian?" Alecia asked.

"Of course I am 'telling tales out of school'," Mrs. Belton said, "but she is Lord Kiniston's 'friend' and it is hardly a secret that she hopes very much to be his wife."

Alecia looked surprised, and Mrs. Belton went on:

"Lady Lillian's husband was killed two years ago before the Battle of Waterloo, and as she is a cousin of Lord Kiniston she has taken over the running of his Château for him and will act as chaperon while you are there."

Alecia wondered if this would make things more difficult than they were already and decided that, if Lord Kiniston was interested in Lady Lillian, perhaps he would pay very little attention to her and she might in fact find it easy to keep out of his way as much as possible.

Mrs. Belton was still chattering on.

"Of course," she was saying, "I do not really admire Lady Lillian myself. She is too exotic for my liking, and I am glad to say my husband thinks the same, but the lady whom the Duke of Wellington finds charming is very different."

"Who is she?" Alecia managed to ask.

"Her name is Mrs. Marianne Patterson," Mrs. Belton replied, delighted to go on talking. "She and her two sisters are American and are known as 'The Three Graces', and I can tell you a lot of other women are very envious of them."

"American!" Alecia exclaimed in surprise.

"Yes, they come from Baltimore and are the great-granddaughters of a multi-millionaire, Charles Caton."

"I have never met an American," Alecia said.

Then she thought perhaps that was an indiscreet

thing to say since Charis was certain to have met quite a number in London.

"Well, I am sure you will find the three sisters very charming," Mrs. Belton said, "but I am rather doubtful about Lady Lillian."

"Now you are making me nervous!" Alecia exclaimed.

Mrs. Belton laughed and said:

"I cannot believe from all I have heard about you, Lady Charis, that anything would make you nervous!"

They reached Dover at about five o'clock and the ship was waiting at the quay-side.

It seemed to Alecia quite large and at the same time she was worried as to whether she would be a good or a bad sailor, having never been to sea before. One thing she had not expected was that with their luggage there were several large wicker hampers, and when she enquired what they were, she was told they contained food.

"Food!" she exclaimed. "But why?"

"We should take only three to five hours crossing the Channel, but we might be becalmed," the Courier explained. "On one of my journeys the Packet was becalmed for three days, and I have known of cases where passengers were forced to stay in the middle of the Channel for up to eleven days."

This was something which had never occurred to Alecia, and instead of hoping for a completely calm sea with no wind, she hoped they would be blown in the right direction as quickly as possible.

As soon as the ship left the quay-side Mrs. Belton went to her cabin, saying she was a bad sailor and could only tolerate the sea when she was lying down.

Alecia found it a relief after so much chatter to be able first of all to watch the ship move out of harbour, then to go to her own cabin where Sarah, her lady's-maid was unpacking everything she would need for the night.

The dinner, at which there was no sign of Mrs. Belton, having been provided by Lord Kiniston, was delicious and to Alecia's mind very rich.

There was *pâté*, cold chicken stuffed in a delicious manner, cutlets of baby lamb covered in aspic, tender and delicately flavoured with herbs.

As dessert there was fresh fruit which she learnt from Mr. Hunt came from Kiniston Hall, and to drink there was a white wine followed by a claret of which Alecia took only a sip, but knew how much her father would have appreciated it.

After she had eaten what she thought was a very large meal she went to bed, and the next morning it was a relief to find she had slept peacefully and was only woken early by the noise on deck.

A little afterwards Mr. Hunt knocked on her door and told her they had crossed the Channel without any difficulties and would be in Calais Harbour in about an hour.

This gave Alecia time to dress, eat the breakfast that was brought to her and be standing on deck to have her first sight of a French town.

Calais did not disappoint her, although Mr. Hunt said scornfully it was not a particularly impressive port.

It was not until they had actually docked that Mrs. Belton appeared looking rather pale, and although she had not been sick she had spent an uncomfortable night disliking every movement of the ship.

There was so much Alecia would have liked to see in the streets of Calais, the people, the children, the tall houses with their shuttered windows, but Mr. Hunt hurried them into carriages that were waiting.

Alecia saw that they had drivers wearing British uniforms and out-riders who were also soldiers, two for each carriage, who went ahead as look-outs in case of any trouble on the road.

Soon Mrs. Belton was feeling well enough to chatter again and Alecia found herself not listening to what she was saying, but looking out of the window.

Having heard so many terrible stories of the plight of France under Napoleon, she was surprised to see how much of the land was being cultivated and how the crops appeared to have been well planted and were springing up in the warm sunshine.

At the same time, she was aware that there were few men, unless they were very old or children, to be seen, and that the work was being done by the women.

'War is wrong and wicked,' she thought, and remembered that Mrs. Belton had warned her not to say such things to Lord Kiniston.

They stayed the night at a posting Inn south of St. Omer and set out very early the next morning so that they would reach their destination by nightfall.

It was, however, dusk before Mrs. Belton exclaimed with satisfaction that they were on the outskirts of Cambrai and in a few minutes would see the Château where Lord Kiniston was staying, which was nearer to them than that of the Duke of Wellington.

It was then that Alecia thought she was stiff from sitting so long and tired of travelling and of Mrs. Belton's unceasing chatter.

She kept saying over and over again how many women had loved Lord Kiniston, which was obviously a subject which fascinated her.

Because the mere idea of him frightened Alecia, she did not want to listen to what he had done, or who had interested him before she actually saw him.

She was still finding it hard to understand why he should have wanted Charis to come out to him in France, making it, in her estimation at any rate, an order which could not be refused.

"If he has Lady Lillian and a number of other women it seems extraordinary that he should bother himself over a young girl who has been his Ward for over a year since her father's death, without his paying any attention to her," Alecia argued.

She supposed when she reached Cambrai she would learn all the answers, but for the moment it all seemed incomprehensible.

Yet now, feeling rather tired after so arduous a journey, she could understand that if Charis had been in her rightful place, she would have resented it as every mile took her further and further away from Harry.

It was like stepping into another world, and leaving behind everything that was familiar.

"I shall have to play my part skilfully, so that Lord Kiniston will never suspect," Alecia told herself.

At the same time, though Charis had told her that when everything was clear she could return, she was going to manage to do so without Lord Kiniston's help.

She had the terrifying feeling that he might be so angry that he would refuse to give her a Courier, or provide her with an Army escort such as she had at the moment.

Mrs. Belton had already related to her horrifying stories of the way travellers in France had been robbed not only of their baggage, but even of their clothes, while the French were still suffering from the food shortage they had endured towards the end of the war when every available man had been called up by Napoleon, and there was no one to see to the crops.

'I am sure somebody will be kind to me,' Alecia thought consolingly.

At the same time, because Charis had made everything sound so easy, she had not anticipated how difficult the journey would be or really how long it would take.

Then, as the sun was sinking on the horizon, turning the sky to gold and crimson, she saw in front of her a very attractive Château.

Surrounded by trees, it was typically French, and in front of it, as they drew a little nearer she could see a formal garden with a fountain playing, its water iridescent in the last rays of the sun.

It was so pretty that she felt after travelling for so long that it was almost a happy omen.

Then she told herself that this was where the real test began, and she had to be very much on her guard and very careful of what she said.

"We are here!" Mrs. Belton said. "I must say, I am not only thankful the journey is over, but I am prepared to say a prayer of gratitude that we have not been involved in any unpleasantness. It is no use your thinking the French like having an Army of Occupation – they dislike it very much!"

"Yes .. of course," Alecia murmured. "I am sure no one .. whoever they may be, wants to be conquered and humiliated."

The carriage drew up outside the Château and at the top of a flight of steps there were a number of servants, while on either side of the steps stood sentries on duty, who presented arms as they stepped out of the carriage.

Mrs. Belton went ahead and at the top of the steps a Senior Servant appeared with an *Aide-de-Camp*.

"It is good to see you, Mrs. Belton," the *Aide-de-Camp* said. "We were afraid you might be delayed, and His Lordship has already gone to dress for dinner."

"I suppose we are a little late," Mrs. Belton replied, "but we are here, and let me present you to Lady Charis Langley."

"I have been looking forward to meeting you, My Lady," the *Aide-de-Camp* smiled.

Alecia seeing the admiration in his eyes and, realising he held her hand a little longer than was necessary, thought that Charis's reputation had obviously preceded her and the *Aide-de-Camp* was thinking of the success she had enjoyed in London.

"I know His Lordship will want to hold back dinner for you, but not for longer than is necessary," the *Aide-de-Camp* was saying. "So I will have you shown immediately to your rooms, and I am sure you will be as quick as is humanly possible in the circumstances."

"We will do our best," Mrs. Belton said, "but I feel as if it will take hours to wash away the dust and grime from the journey!"

The Housekeeper appeared at the top of the stairs and having curtsied to them politely, a little lower to Alecia than to Mrs. Belton, she led them to their rooms.

Almost immediately the luggage was brought upstairs. As Alecia bathed, the new maid, with whom she had exchanged only a few words on board ship, found her a gown to wear that had not been crushed by the journey.

There was another maid to assist her own, and yet another to prepare a bath scented with verbena in which Alecia would have liked to lie luxuriously to soak away the fatigue of the journey.

But she knew she must do nothing of the sort unless she wished to offend her Guardian before she had even met him.

She was perceptive enough to realise from the way the *Aide-de-Camp* had spoken, and the haste with which they had been escorted upstairs, that His Lordship did not like waiting for his meals, and resented if they were in fact delayed for even a short time.

'I must hurry!' Alecia thought.

She felt it would have been far more sensible if she and Mrs. Belton could have retired to bed, and she could have faced what was waiting for her tomorrow.

Instead she was helped into one of the prettiest gowns she possessed, her hair was skilfully arranged in the style which Charis had told her was the very latest fashion, and carrying a reticule to match her gown, she hurried downstairs escorted by a servant who had been waiting for her outside her door until she was ready.

Now was the moment which she had feared ever since leaving home would be frightening and extremely embarrassing.

"I have to remember I am Charis," she told herself.

As she walked across the marble hall she was praying that she would not make any mistakes, nor appear as she felt, shy and a little gauche.

"I am Charis! I am Charis!" she said over and over again.

The Major Domo who had taken over from the servant who had led her down the stairs walked ahead to fling open the doors leading to what Alecia guessed would be the most important Salon in the Château.

"Lady Charis Langley, M'Lord!" he announced in stentorian tones.

For a moment everything swam in front of Alecia's eyes and the room seemed to be full of people, so that it was impossible to distinguish anyone amongst them.

Then a man detached himself slowly from those who stood around the fireplace at the far end and moved towards her under the light of the crystal chandeliers. She saw someone very tall, broad-shouldered, and knew this was Lord Kiniston, her supposed Guardian.

It took her a moment to raise her eyes and focus them on his face.

He was quite different from what she had expected, and yet at the same time exactly how Charis had thought he would be, and Mrs. Belton had described him.

Overwhelming, authoritative, with a sharp and penetrating eye, to Alecia's mind, definitely very frightening.

CHAPTER THREE

Some ten days before Alecia's arrival in Cambrai Lord Kiniston was sitting writing at a desk in an attractive small Salon which overlooked the garden when the door opened.

He glanced up, then gave an exclamation of delight as he said:

"You are back, Willy! Thank God for that!"

Major William Lygon came into the Salon shutting the door behind him.

He was a tall, good-looking man, with a somewhat raffish air, and twinkling eyes which endeared him to everybody he met.

"Yes, I am back, Drogo," he said. "Has anything exciting happened while I have been away?"

"Nothing," Lord Kiniston replied, moving from behind the desk to stand in front of the marble fireplace while Major Lygon lowered himself into a comfortable armchair.

"I can hardly believe that," he said as he did so, "but you missed a great deal of amusement in London, and I am not particularly excited about being back in this God-forsaken place!"

"There is plenty of work for you to do," Lord Kiniston remarked laconically. "The Great Man has been tightening things up because the French have complained that some of our men are unruly."

"Good God, can you blame them?" Willy Lygon asked. "But you will be glad to hear that I travelled with four couples of hounds and a spaniel for the Duke's collection, and I am told that three stags and three does will be on their way in a week."

"Good Lord!" Lord Kiniston ejaculated. "At the same time I hear that he is determined on having boar hunts based on the principles of pig sticking, at which he excelled while he was in India."

"What more can you ask for?" Willy Lygon enquired sarcastically.

"I can only ask that the Great Man will confine himself to sport."

The way Lord Kiniston spoke and the innuendo in his voice made his friend look at him curiously.

They had been at Eton together and after a short time at Oxford had joined the same Regiment on the same day.

But Lord Kiniston had swept up the ladder of success far quicker than William Lygon, who had not worried about it in the least.

He liked life to be comfortable and was too good-humoured to envy anyone or, for that matter, to get involved in a quarrel of any sort.

He had a deep affection for Drogo Kiniston and now he looked at him curiously as he asked:

"What has the Great Man been doing to you?"

"Trying to get me married!" Lord Kiniston said frankly.

Willy sat upright in his armchair.

"I do not believe it!"

"It is true!"

"But – why? And to whom?"

Lord Kiniston paused for a moment before he replied:

"You will remember before you went away that he was obviously infatuated with Marianne Patterson?"

"Yes, of course," Willy murmured.

"Well, in his usual manner of giving advice and helping pretty women, which we all realise has become one of his pleasures, he has vowed to find husbands for her two unmarried sisters."

"And he has chosen you as a bridegroom?" Willy asked mockingly. "I do not believe it!"

"He is making it pretty obvious that he expects me to propose to Elizabeth," Lord Kiniston replied, "and Louisa is being reserved for Felton-Hervey."

"Do you mean to say the perfect *Aide-de-Camp* is going to be caught at last?"

"I think so," Lord Kiniston replied seriously. "With the Duke pushing him hard he will find it very difficult to escape."

"And what are you going to do about it?"

"I was hoping you could tell me that," Lord Kiniston answered. "I suppose you do not feel like entering the matrimonial stakes yourself?"

"I do not!" Willy said firmly. "Besides, the 'Three Graces' would not consider me distinguished or rich enough. I was told confidentially that each one of them is determined to win a coronet."

"Hervey will have one eventually," Lord Kiniston remarked.

"And you have one already, which will be one up for Elizabeth, if she pulls it off!"

"Dammit all!" Lord Kiniston said angrily. "I will not be forced up the aisle by anybody, not even the

Great Man himself! If the worst comes to the worst, I shall resign!"

"You cannot do that!" Willy said quickly. "I was told the moment I got back that there is increasing hostility towards the Occupation, and I also heard that King Louis implored Wellington to remain in Paris, when he was there, as a prop to his Government."

"I heard that too," Lord Kiniston answered, "but the British Cabinet thinks he is safer here at Cambrai."

"I suppose that is true," Willy said reflectively.

"Personally, I think they are fussing unnecessarily," Lord Kiniston replied. "The Duke said to me the other day that he wished the British Cabinet would put aside the idea that he was anxious to be assassinated by a French mob."

"Well, nobody wants that," Willy smiled, "and if there is any chance of the Duke or you being attacked, then you must stay here, dull though it may be. By the way, how is Lady Lillian?"

There was a perceptible pause before Lord Kiniston replied:

"Quite frankly, Willy, I am beginning to think she is out-staying her welcome."

Willy Lygon raised his eyebrows.

He had thought before he left for England that his friend's *affaire de coeur* with the beautiful Lady Lillian would eventually end in the permanency of marriage.

He told himself now it was not surprising that Drogo was bored.

Women clung to him, pressed him too hard, and tried to tie him down with every wile in their repertoire.

It was not surprising therefore that his love-affairs, if that was the right word for them, never lasted for very long.

Whenever a woman became possessive, Lord Kiniston became restless, and then it was only a question of time before there were tears, recriminations, reproaches and accusations, which inevitably left him unmoved.

"I can see you have got your affairs in somewhat of a mess!" Willy said wryly. "I suppose, if the truth were told, Lady Lillian is jealous of Elizabeth Caton and afraid that the Duke may get his way and she will lose you completely."

"You would think I was the only man in the world!" Lord Kiniston remarked bitterly, which made his friend laugh.

"I have another problem," he said after a moment, "and one on which you may be able to help me."

"What is it?"

Lord Kiniston walked across to his desk and picking up a letter walked back to the fireplace before he said:

"This is from the Solicitors of the late Earl of Langhaven. Do you remember him?"

"Yes, of course, I rather liked him. He was a good soldier."

Lord Kiniston did not reply, but was looking down at the letter. Then he said:

"I had, in fact, forgotten about it, until his Solicitors wrote to me a year ago on his death, but he left me as the Guardian of his daughter."

"His daughter!" Willy exclaimed. "You do not mean to say you are the Guardian of 'Aphrodite'?"

Lord Kiniston raised his head.

"Are you referring to Lady Charis Langley?"

"Of course I am," Willy replied. "She is the most talked about, the most admired young woman in the whole of London. All I can say, Drogo, is that, if you

49

are her Guardian, you might have introduced me to her."

"I have never seen the girl. In fact, I had never heard of her except on her father's death."

"Then let me tell you about her," Willy said. "I have only seen her in the distance – but she is really lovely and every man who meets her throws his heart at her feet."

"How very dramatic!" Lord Kiniston remarked sarcastically.

"She was an instantaneous success when she appeared in London last Season," Willy went on. "In fact, marooned as I was out here, I was sick to death of hearing about her attractions and charm. Then her father died and she was in mourning when I went back on leave this time and found they were still talking about her! The Betting-Book at White's is filled with wagers on which of the most notorious fortune-hunters will carry her off as a prize."

"Fortune-hunters?" Lord Kiniston questioned.

"She is not only beautiful, but she is also rich," Willy said, "and few impoverished young aristocrats can re-sist such an obvious bait."

"That explains what is in this letter."

"Read it to me."

"As I have said, it is from the Langhaven Solicitors, and they say that, since as I did not reply to the last letter they wrote to me on the death of their revered client, they have carried on supervising Lady Charis's affairs to the best of their ability."

Lord Kiniston raised his eyes and looked at his friend.

"But they are slightly perturbed by the fact that she has asked them to release £20,000 of her fortune, as she wishes to set up a racing-stable. They think in the circumstances they should ask my approval before agreeing to such a very large demand."

"£20,000!" Willy exclaimed. "I wonder who is taking that off her?"

Lord Kiniston did not speak and after a moment Willy continued:

"It might be Parkington – I know he is 'below hatches', and Hexton as you know, has been complaining for years that his ancestral home is literally tumbling down. Both of them are in the Book at White's."

"And they are both of them young wasters!" Lord Kiniston said sharply. "Parkington gambles too high, and Hexton drinks to excess!"

"Perhaps 'Aphrodite' will reform whichever one she chooses," Willy suggested blithely.

Then he gave an exclamation.

"I have an idea, Drogo!"

"What is it?" Lord Kiniston asked.

"Why do you not invite your Ward to come here? It would be a good idea for you to meet her, and with 'Aphrodite' in the house, the Great Man might think it impossible for even one of the Graces to attract your attention."

Lord Kiniston stared at his friend in surprise. Then he said:

"Are you really suggesting .. ?"

"You are her Guardian," Willy interrupted, "and I suppose she cannot marry without your approval unless she is over twenty-one."

"No, of course not!" Lord Kiniston agreed as if the idea had only just occurred to him.

"By the way," Willy said, "why on earth should

Langhaven have made you the girl's Guardian in the first place?"

Lord Kiniston smiled, and it softened the hard expression on his face.

"It was just after the Armistice when we joined the Regiment. I dare say you have forgotten it, but I got a great deal more ragging than you did because my father had died and the newspapers had reported what I had inherited in such glowing terms that you would have thought I was Croesus!"

"I remember that," Willy said.

"And do you also remember that before we went into our first battle in Portugal old Schofield, who commanded us in those days, told us all to make our Wills. I always thought it was a ghoulish thing to do, making it clear that he expected some, if not all, of us to be killed."

"I was not with you when that happened," Willy said. "I had been sent abroad to reconnoitre the position of the enemy, a mission almost impossible in the dark!"

"I had forgotten that," Lord Kiniston answered. "Well, what happened was that we did as we were told and sat down to write out our Wills, and Langley, who had not then come into the title, came into the room and said:

"'I have been told to suggest to you, gentlemen, that you take this seriously and appoint for your children, if you have any, a responsible Guardian, who will look after them if anything should happen to your wife.'

"He spoke seriously, but there was a twinkle in his eye as most of the officers were unmarried, and the rest had distinguished relatives who would obviously be conscious of their responsibilities.

52

"Then as Langley and I sat down at a table together, he said:

"'Personally, I can think of no one important or rich enough to take care of my daughter. Do you think the Queen would accept the position?'

"There was laughter at this, then somebody, I have forgotten who it was, said:

"'Why not appoint young Kiniston? We all know how rich he is, and he is certainly distinguished enough to make an admirable Guardian!'"

"So that is how it happened!" Willy exclaimed.

"I never gave it another thought," Lord Kiniston went on, "until a year ago when on Langhaven's death his Solicitors wrote to me to say that I was the Guardian of his daughter, and I realised he had never made another Will."

"And you did not reply?"

"No. I was very busy at the time, and afterwards it slipped my mind, until this letter arrived yesterday."

"Well, I have told you what to do about it."

"Of course your idea is ridiculous!" Lord Kiniston exclaimed.

Then he was silent and Willy, watching him, knew he was in fact, thinking it over.

"At the same time," he said after a moment, "the Great Man has made it very obvious what he required of me."

"And Lady Lillian is being difficult," Willy added.

"I will do as you say!" Lord Kiniston exclaimed suddenly. "Anyway, £20,000 is far too much money for a young woman to throw away on a fortune-hunter! Most of them do not know a good horse from a bad."

"You are right there," Willy agreed. "But if she is

setting up a racing-stable with that amount of money, I would not mind participating in it myself!"

Lord Kiniston did not say any more, he merely sat down at the desk, and wrote two letters, the first to the Solicitors to say he would deal with their query in due course, and the second to the Ward he had never seen, Lady Charis Langley.

When he had given the letters to an Orderly to send to England with the despatches that left Wellington's Headquarters every day for London, Lady Lillian came into the room.

She was an extremely attractive woman and used her looks as a bait to catch any man she fancied.

From the moment she had seen her distant cousin, Lord Kiniston, she had been determined to enslave him, and had only been prevented for some two years from achieving her objective because both her cousin and her husband were fighting in the Peninsula.

Then George Somerset was most conveniently killed, and when she learnt that Drogo Kiniston was in Paris setting up the Army of Occupation with the Duke of Wellington, she had left immediately for the French Capital and for a short time had managed to be a guest in the Duke's mansion on the Champs Élysées.

After that it was quite easy for her to move with Lord Kiniston to Cambrai, and install herself in his Château.

By this time he had found her not only useful in various ways, but also extremely attractive as a woman.

In fact, in all the many love-affairs in which he had indulged whenever he was not on the battlefield, he had never known a woman so passionate and so insatiable.

Looking at her now as she came into the Salon, her

eyes slanting a little at the corners, which gave her a mysterious look, and her red lips pouting provocatively because she thought she was being neglected, Willy thought it would be difficult for any woman to look more exotic and seductive.

And yet, knowing Drogo Kiniston as well as he did, he was aware as Lady Lillian went to his side and reached out her long slender fingers to touch him that he stiffened as if he resented her intimacy.

"How can you have neglected me for so long, dearest Drogo?" Lady Lillian asked. "I have been waiting for hours for you in the Salon, but I was told you were in conference and thought you had a number of officers here."

"Only Willy," Lord Kiniston replied.

Rather slowly Willy rose from his armchair as Lady Lillian turned to look at him.

"So you are back!" she said in a somewhat uncompromising voice.

"Yes, I am back, Lady Lillian," Willy replied, "and, of course, delighted to see you again and looking as usual like a ray of sunshine."

There was always a sarcastic note in Willy's voice when he paid her a compliment, and Lady Lillian always resented it because she knew he was mocking her.

She was well aware that he did not like her, and although she tried to put it down merely to jealousy because of his long friendship with Drogo Kiniston, she knew it was something more than that, and hated him for it.

"Well, nobody informed me," she said, "that you were coming back today! I am supposed to be running this house for dear Drogo, and it may be inconvenient to put you up."

"That is quite all right," Willy replied. "My favourite room has been kept for me, and, as I expect you are aware, most of my worldly possessions are still in it."

Knowing that she could not refuse to accept him, Lady Lillian shrugged her shoulders and looking up at Lord Kiniston in a way he invariably found irresistible said:

"Dearest Drogo, when you have time after luncheon, will you take me for a short drive? I seem to have been cooped up in this house for days without a chance of being alone with you."

As Lord Kiniston had spent most of the previous night with her, this was of course untrue.

But she hoped he would appreciate the way she was keeping their liaison secret from Willy.

"I am afraid this afternoon is impossible," Lord Kiniston replied. "The Duke required me to be with him at two o'clock, so we must have luncheon early."

Lady Lillian gave a little cry.

"In which case I must go and give the order, otherwise you might be late and that, as you well know, would be disastrous!"

She reached the door, then turned back to say:

"I suppose he wishes to see you on Army business? It is not just an excuse for you to entertain those Caton girls without my being invited?"

"I am looking forward to seeing the 'Three Graces' again," Willy remarked, knowing his interest would annoy Lady Lillian.

"You will not have to look far for them," she said tartly. "They hang around the dear Duke like strands

56

of clinging ivy. Marianne Patterson actually persuaded him to take her to see the field of Waterloo!"

"I am surprised that he agreed to that," Willy said.

"It was extremely selfish of her," Lady Lillian replied, "and she confessed afterwards that had she realised the mental anguish the sight caused him she would never have proposed such a visit."

"I should think not," Willy agreed, "for we all know he hates to talk about it, let alone see it."

"It was a great mistake," Lord Kiniston agreed, "and something which must not be repeated."

"I am sure you, Drogo dear, will see to that."

Lady Lillian gave him a dazzling smile before she left the room, leaving behind her the fragrance of a French perfume and for a moment there was silence between the two friends.

At length Willy said:

"She is very much the Chatelaine of the Château. You will have great difficulty in getting her to move elsewhere."

"I may have to go to Paris myself," Lord Kiniston remarked.

Again there was a pause. Then as if he wished to change the subject he said:

"By the way, there is somebody I want you to meet who actually is the owner of this house."

Willy looked surprised.

"I thought it belonged to the *Duc* de St. Briere."

"It does," Lord Kiniston said.

"You know him?"

"He was here a week ago to see the Duke, and also to see how I was looking after his Château."

"What is he like?"

"He seems very charming," Lord Kiniston replied.

"He is of course one of the 'Old Régime'. He loathes Napoleon whom he refers to as 'that Corsican upstart,' and says that he is delighted we have beaten him. In consequence he is only too delighted for me to occupy this house, which he told me was comprehensively looted in the Revolution."

"I should have thought he was fortunate not to have lost his head!" Willy remarked.

"Apparently he escaped from Paris, finally reaching England to spend a great deal of the war in London and Brighton."

"With a large number of other *émigrés*," Willy intervened.

"Exactly!" Lord Kiniston agreed. "And I understand that he was useful towards the end of the war when he returned to France in disguise and helped the British against the Napoleonic Army."

"That was brave of him," Willy replied, "and I would like to meet him."

"I have invited him to dinner tonight," Lord Kiniston said, "and you can tell me what you think of him."

"You sound as if you yourself are a little doubtful," Willy suggested.

"Shall I say I am not absolutely sure," Lord Kiniston replied, "but Lady Lillian is delighted with him and so are several other women."

"All Frenchmen have that 'kiss the hand, and look with eloquent eyes' technique which English women love," Willy remarked.

Lord Kiniston laughed.

"You are quite right, Willy, and it is an art that we as a race have no intention of acquiring. Come and have a look at the horses. I have bought a new charger, which will make you envious."

"Am I ever anything else where you are concerned?" Willy asked. "It is not only that you are too rich, but you are too knowledgeable, especially where horses and women are concerned!"

Lord Kiniston did not answer but put his arm through Willy's and they walked into the hall.

He thought that he would enjoy having his friend back far more if it were not for Lillian pressurising him, and the Duke continually extolling the attractions of Elizabeth Caton.

Over the next week it seemed to Lord Kiniston that things were accelerating in an unpleasant manner which he could not control.

The Duke was obviously convinced that there was no one more suitable as a husband for his protégée Elizabeth.

Because Lady Lillian would have been extremely foolish if she had not realised what was afoot, she clung desperately to her position in her cousin's life.

She also made it abundantly clear that after she had given him what women call 'their all', he should do the right thing and marry her.

Lord Kiniston found himself fighting against her persistence which increased day by day.

He spent as much time as he could with the troops and on horseback.

He could not, however, without being extremely rude, refuse the countless dinner-parties that were arranged for the Duke of Wellington and at which, as his Second-in-Command, he was expected to be present.

In the meantime, the political difficulties arising from the Occupation did not lessen.

France was complaining that it was impossible to

feed the hundred and fifty thousand men of the Army of Occupation and began to press the Duke to send home at least thirty thousand immediately.

The Duke was in a dilemma which did not make him any easier to be with.

It seemed that only Marianne Patterson could bring a smile to his lips and a tender expression to his rather tired eyes.

As Lord Kiniston was well aware, Marianne had her own axe to grind.

She was determined – and she was in fact, under a soft, feminine, and attractive exterior, a very determined woman – that her two sisters should make brilliant marriages which would astound their friends in Baltimore.

The Duke believed that in pressing first his favourite *Aide-de-Camp* and then Lord Kiniston, to marry two of the most charming girls he had ever met, he was doing them a good turn.

He was not concerned that Lord Kiniston was obviously resisting such a suggestion, for he took it for granted that at thirty-three it was time his Second-in-Command settled down, and that when the Occupation came to an end, he would leave the Army and retire to look after his huge estates in Berkshire.

The Duke had seen Kiniston Hall, and had been extremely impressed by it, and he knew that any American would find the great house, which had been built by Robert Adam, irresistible.

He therefore talked about it to Elizabeth Caton, and was aware that in her eyes, Lord Kiniston seemed surrounded by an aura of glamour that would have been less appealing to any English girl.

"I have done my best for the boy," Wellington said to himself.

He always thought of his officers as 'my boys', and they could never be entirely supplanted in his imagination even by his own sons.

In fact, the Duke of Wellington's ideal life was an Army Mess, and his ideal family the 'Military Family' of his *Aides-de-Camp*.

Being unhappily married, he wanted to play 'Cupid' to other men, and like all authoritative personalities he thought he knew what was best for other people.

Lord Kiniston who had sized him up the first moment he met him, was aware that this was a great danger where he was concerned.

He had no wish to quarrel with the man he admired above all others, or to have any animosity between himself and his Commanding Officer.

At the same time, he had evaded marriage up until now with a skill and adroitness that had made him feel that he was too wily a fish, and far too clever ever to be caught.

Now he knew the net was closing in.

If he was not careful, it would be a choice between Lillian, who had already begun to bore him, or a young American girl with whom he had nothing in common.

He was quite certain that she too would bore him to extinction within a few months of their being married.

"What shall I do? What the devil shall I do?" he asked himself at night when he went to bed.

The problem haunted him as soon as he awoke every morning, and although he tried to evade it, it was with him all day.

It was with a feeling of relief therefore that he received a letter from his secretary.

It was as if being in a beleaguered fortress he had learnt that a relieving Army was on its way to his rescue.

His secretary wrote that arrangements had been made for Lady Charis Langley to arrive at Cambrai on the day he had chosen, accompanied by Mrs. Belton.

He was not quite certain how it would all work out: he just knew, and here his intuition and imagination had begun to work, that he had taken the right action at the right time.

Lord Kiniston would not have been so brilliant a commander on the battlefield, if he had used only his mind in command of his men and not also his intuition.

Sometimes he was aware of danger long before it actually happened. At other times he was confident of victory when everybody else was envisaging defeat.

Now he felt as he heard the Major Domo's voice announce: "Lady Charis Langley, M'Lord!" as if it was a trumpet-call of victory.

As he walked slowly across the room he realised that everything Willy had said about her beauty was true and she was in fact quite one of the loveliest young women he had ever seen in his life.

Then as he said:

"It is delightful to welcome you, Lady Charis, and I am glad you have got here safely," he took her hand in his.

As he did so, he was aware that her fingers quivered in a way he could not understand, and when he looked into her large and very beautiful eyes, he saw to his astonishment that she was afraid.

For a moment he thought he must be mistaken, then

because he was very experienced where women were concerned, he knew she was not pretending, but was definitely frightened.

"I must introduce you to my friends," he said, but he did not for the moment relinquish her hand and he had the feeling, although he might have been mistaken, that she clung to him as if for support.

Then as he introduced her first to Lady Lillian, who gushed an insincere welcome, then to several other guests, he was still surprised that she seemed unsure of herself, and only Willy was able to make her give a soft, musical little laugh.

"Lady Charis, I have been stalking you for years," he said, "and now at last, when I am respectably and conventionally introduced to you, it is the most exciting moment of my life!"

His words sounded so strange to Alecia, who had never been paid a compliment, that she laughed and Willy said insistently:

"It is the truth! I have seen you once in London and I have prayed fervently ever since that I might one day meet you and talk to you."

"It is .. very .. kind of you to be so .. flattering," Alecia said.

She had been afraid when Lord Kiniston started to introduce her to everybody that there might be somebody there who knew Charis fairly well.

She had never for a moment imagined there would be a large dinner-party of fashionable people the very night she arrived in Cambrai.

She had somehow thought that she would be alone in the house with perhaps just Mrs. Belton as a chaperon.

When finally the Major's wife came hurrying into the room full of apologies for being late, Alecia realised

63

that there were fourteen people for dinner, and quite a number of them were staying in the house.

Mrs. Belton had warned her that Lady Lillian was hostess to Lord Kiniston, and she herself had also made it very clear to Alecia who was in charge.

"I hope," she said when dinner was over, "that you are comfortable in your room, Lady Charis. I chose one which has the early morning sun, as I felt that was what you would appreciate, and of course, it is one of the best rooms in the house."

"That is . . very kind of you," Alecia managed to say.

Lady Lillian went on:

"If there is anything you want, you must tell *me*. I try to prevent my dear cousin from having to trouble himself over small domestic matters which men always find so boring."

Alecia did not speak and she went on:

"Of course I shall do my best to find you suitably charming and attentive young men to amuse you while you are here, but I am afraid your Guardian is a very busy man, and so conscientious that he seldom has time for anything but work."

She did not realise, Alecia thought, that the one thing that would best please her would be to have as little to do with her so-called 'Guardian' as possible.

She thought that even if she had not listened to Mrs. Belton's gossip, she would have suspected Lady Lillian of being very close and intimate with Lord Kiniston.

When the gentlemen joined the ladies after dinner Lady Lillian went to his side and engaged him in a very confidential conversation which could not be over-heard by anybody else.

Although it was obvious he wanted to talk to his other guests also, she was always near him, listening to what he said and making the conversation, whenever it was possible, centre on herself.

'I do not like her!' Alecia thought.

She herself was listening rather than talking and, as if he realised it, Willy came to sit beside her and say:

"I expect you are tired after your long journey, but I have been waiting to hear the witty remarks with which you are credited in London, and which I suspect are often at someone else's expense."

"I hope not," Alecia replied. "I would not wish to be unkind to anyone here when they have all been so kind to me."

"You really think that?" Willy asked.

He could not help as he spoke having a quick glance at Lady Lillian who was looking in their direction, at the same time standing so near to Lord Kiniston that her arm was touching his.

Because she was afraid that she would make some *faux pas* and give herself away by mistake, Alecia said:

"I wonder if it would be possible for me to go to bed? It has been a very long day, and I am feeling rather tired."

"Of course. I am sure you can!" Willy said. "It is just because you are so beautiful that no one for a moment will believe that you need any 'beauty sleep'!"

"Do you talk to everybody like that?" Alecia asked.

"Like what?" Willy asked.

"Paying them compliments to which it is difficult to find an answer."

Willy laughed, and it was a spontaneous sound.

As he did so Lord Kiniston came up to them to ask:

"What is amusing you, Willy?

"Lady Charis is being unkind to me," Willy complained. "You will hardly believe it, Drogo, but she does not appreciate my compliments."

"I was not . . complaining," Alecia said quickly, "it is just that they seem . . very exaggerated!"

"*I* am sure they are," Lord Kiniston said. "You should learn a lesson from the French, Willy, and be more subtle."

"Now *you* are being unkind to me!" Willy grumbled, but his eyes were twinkling. Then he added:

"Actually, Lady Charis is anxious to go to bed. I expect she is finding us 'country bumpkins' rather dull after all the glamour and excitement that she enjoys in London."

"No, no . . of course not . . that is not . . true!" Alecia exclaimed.

Then she realised he was not being serious, and she looked up at Lord Kiniston saying:

"Please . . if it does not seem rude . . I am very tired."

"But of course," he said. "There is no need to say goodnight to everybody, just come with me, which I am sure you would prefer to causing a disturbance."

"Yes, please. I would not want to upset anybody," Alecia said hastily.

They walked across the room, and although Lady Lillian watched them go, she did not say anything.

Lord Kiniston opened the door leading into the hall, and Alecia saw there were rows of silver candle-sticks all containing unlighted candles at the bottom of the stairs.

Lord Kiniston lit a candle and handed it to her, and as she took it from him she curtsied and he said:

"Sleep well, Lady Charis. Tomorow we will have a talk about the reason why I have brought you here, but I am sure for the moment you are very tired."

"Yes, I am," Alecia agreed.

As she looked up at him he realised there was still an expression of fear in her eyes, and as she turned her head away, he knew she was shy.

She walked up the stairs, and he watched her, knowing that as every other woman did, when she reached the top she would turn back to look down at him and say 'goodnight'.

But Alecia walked on, holding her candle carefully, and with her head bent.

As she disappeared from sight Lord Kiniston stood thinking that she was very different from what Willy had said about her.

"She is lovely!" he told himself. "But what, in God's name, is making her afraid?"

CHAPTER FOUR

As soon as the dinner-guests had left Lord Kiniston retired to bed.

He was worried about his own position, but he found himself thinking as he undressed of Charis, and how strange it was that anyone with her reputation of being a social personality should be afraid.

"What can have upset her?" he asked himself and remembered too how she had seemed shy, not only when she arrived, but also when she had gone upstairs to bed.

She was certainly, he thought, very beautiful in an unusual sort of way.

As he was used to sophisticated and very experienced women, he was not prepared for a white skin which hardly needed a touch of powder or lips that had obviously not used the crimson salve with which Lady Lillian and other women adorned their faces.

He thought too there was something touchingly young about Charis.

He supposed it was because he had not met many young girls; if fact, when he thought about it, the Caton sisters were the first he had known at all intimately.

Being American, both Elizabeth and Louisa were

very self-assured, and he had never known either of them to show even the slightest sign of shyness.

They teased the younger officers in a way which no English women would have attempted and appeared very much at their ease, even with the Duke himself.

"I like spirited young women," the Great Man had said on several occasions, and Lord Kiniston had thought that was the right word to describe them.

There was however nothing spirited about Charis, and he was sure she was as gentle as the softness of her musical voice.

What puzzled him was that after all her social success in London she seemed embarrassed when she was paid compliments, except for Willy's, which were so obvious as to be a joke.

Once during the evening he was sure when one of the Subalterns was talking to her that he saw her blushing.

'She is certainly an enigma,' he thought to himself as his valet left him and he got into bed.

He had chosen what was obviously the *Duc's* room in the Château for himself because it was the most important Stateroom and the best furnished.

It also had a large bed draped with red satin curtains, and the *Duc's* coat of arms was embroidered above the headpiece.

Lord Kiniston lay back against his pillows and found himself still thinking of Charis.

He was aware that Lillian would be waiting for him but, for some reason he did not wish to explain to himself, he had no desire to visit her tonight.

When he told Willy that she had outstayed her welcome he meant it.

Because he liked organising things it irked him to

have anyone giving orders in his house and arranging everything in the way they thought best, rather than what he wanted himself.

When he had first come to Cambrai there had been so much to do in housing the troops, seeing they were properly fed and keeping them occupied so that they did not encroach on the French population, that he had been glad to let Lillian have things her own way.

Now he knew it had been a mistake.

He had not thought then that she would be determined to marry him, and her first step would be to establish herself as the Chatelaine of his house and the hostess whom everybody would treat as if she was already his wife.

'I must get rid of her somehow,' Lord Kiniston thought and knew that really the most effective way would be to give in to the Duke and marry Elizabeth Caton.

Then he knew that would be equally disastrous and so utterly alien to everything he wanted, that he shied away from the idea like a nervous horse.

"I will not marry anyone!" he said aloud.

As he spoke the door opened and Lillian came in, and for a moment he stared at her incredulously.

It had always been understood that he approached her at night, and it was in fact an unwritten law in an *affaire de coeur* that the woman was pursued by the man, especially when it concerned the bedroom.

This was palpably untrue in many ways, and yet when it came to the sexual enjoyment of two people, there were very few women, however brazen, who would go to a man's bedroom rather than wait for him to come to hers.

Lillian was looking very alluring as she moved sensuously towards the bed, her negligee as diaphanous as her nightgown beneath it.

Despite frills of lace and bows of velvet, it was impossible not to be aware that she had a perfect body which offered everything that any man could desire.

Lord Kiniston looked up at her coldly as her eyes glinted in the candlelight.

"Why are you here, Lillian?" he asked.

His voice was hard and there was an expression in his eyes that would have been awe-inspiring to anyone less persistent than Lillian.

"I wanted to talk to you, Drogo."

"I think it is rather too late for that," he replied. "I have had a long day and quite frankly, I am tired."

"Poor darling," she murmured. "In that case I will just kiss you goodnight and let you go to sleep."

She bent forward as she spoke and too late Lord Kiniston realised he should have prevented her from touching him.

Her lips were hungry and very demanding and because she was exceedingly experienced in igniting desire in any man she herself desired, Lord Kiniston finally succumbed to the fire that consumed her.

While his body responded, his mind was still critically aloof and berating him for being a fool.

Only when dawn broke and Lillian left him, slipping away with a smile on her lips and the belief that he was hers, did Lord Kiniston find himself determined that he could not allow this to continue.

He was aware as he had never been before in his life that he wanted very much more from a woman than a physical passion and he knew that Lillian only appealed to what was least estimable in his character.

He knew it was his own fault that he had become involved, which did not make the situation any better.

As the first fingers of light appeared beneath the curtains he told himself that he would not marry Lillian, although she was confident he would do so, and somehow he would rid himself of her completely.

Because he was exceedingly strong and kept himself athletically fit, Lord Kiniston after only a few hours' sleep was not tired, and rose from his bed when his valet called him without any regrets.

He knew the Duke was expecting him at his Château and had asked him to breakfast so that they could discuss the request of the French for the repatriation of thirty thousand soldiers from the Army of Occupation.

He arrived at exactly two minutes to eight looking exceedingly smart in his uniform and very alert.

The Duke, as might be expected, descended from his bedroom at exactly one minute to eight, and having greeted Lord Kiniston walked into the Dining-Room with him.

One of the things the Duke enjoyed was having a confidential discussion at breakfast. Some of his officers after a night of hard drinking or of feminine companionship found this a painful ordeal.

There were no servants present but a number of dishes were set out, English-fashion, on the sideboard.

Lord Kiniston helped himself to veal cutlets, cooked by a French Chef whose sauces were superb.

The Duke immediately embarked on the problem as to whether it would be safe to dispense with thirty thousand men of the occupying forces.

The Russians were playing for French favours, and it was crucial to decide whether or not the French people were basically loyal to the new régime.

"It will mean your going to London for discussions, Your Grace," Lord Kiniston remarked.

"I would not object to that," the Duke replied. "In fact, I think I am in need of a change, and I would rather like to visit Cheltenham. The water there is very efficacious and the doctors know their business."

Looking at him, Lord Kiniston thought that the change would do him good.

He was quite certain that the strain of last year, and his unending negotiations with the French Government, had been very fatiguing.

He murmured something sympathetic and the Duke said:

"Now let us talk about something else – you, for instance, my boy."

Lord Kiniston realised what danger confronted him, in what the Duke was about to say, and he therefore said quickly:

"By the way, Your Grace, I do not know whether you have been told, but my Ward, Lady Charis Langley, arrived last night from England."

"Lady Charis Langley?" the Duke repeated. "You cannot mean the young woman who was such a social success when I was last in England that she commanded more attention, I believe, than I did myself!"

Lord Kiniston laughed.

"I am sure that is impossible! At the same time, I think we are speaking of the same person and you will find her very beautiful and very charming."

"I shall certainly look forward to meeting her," the Duke said, "but surely Lady Charis must be engaged to be married by this time? I was told that she had at least half the Peerage on their knees."

"I am hoping she has refused them all," Lord Kiniston

said. "Her father who, as you know, died a year ago, made me her Guardian, and I have no intention of allowing anyone so attractive to marry a fortune-hunter."

The Duke looked at Lord Kiniston piercingly, then after a moment's pause he said:

"Are you telling me, my boy, that you intend to marry this girl yourself?"

It was then that Lord Kiniston decided on what seemed the only means of extracting himself from what he knew only too well the Duke had in mind for him.

He hesitated, then said in a deprecating manner:

"For the moment it is of course a secret, but . . "

"My dear boy, I had no idea!" the Duke exclaimed. "In fact, as you must know, I was hoping that you would marry Elizabeth Caton, But of course, if you are promised to the beautiful Lady Charis, then there is nothing I can do about it."

"I am afraid not," Lord Kiniston said with a smile.

"Of course I congratulate you," the Duke went on, "and I remember now hearing that Langhaven, whom I always found an excellent officer, left her a lot of money – not that that would matter to you."

"I must beg Your Grace not to mention this to anyone else," Lord Kiniston said, "and I feel sure I can rely on you."

"Of course, my boy, of course!" the Duke said. "But I do not mind admitting I am disappointed, and I know that Mrs. Patterson, who admires you very much, will be extremely sad not to have you as her brother-in-law."

"I feel sure you will be able to find Elizabeth Caton somebody just as suitable," Lord Kiniston said blithely.

When he left the Duke he was aware that he had had a narrow escape.

He was quite sure the Great Man was going to say bluntly and forcefully that he expected him to marry Elizabeth Caton.

In which case, he would either have had to agree, or else face what would probably have been a disagreeable, even acrimonious argument.

"I was clever over that," he told himself.

At the same time he was uncomfortably aware that his decision might be a shock to Charis.

With a twist of his lips he told himself that however beautiful she might be and however much a success, she would not have many suitors of equal standing to himself even though, as the Duke had said, half the Peerage were on their knees before her.

Lord Kiniston was not a conceited man, but he was well aware that his family and title were both very old. His father's position at Court and that of his grandfather and great-grandfather before him, gave him privileges that were not accorded to other men, even though their titles were superior to his in the aristocratic hierarchy.

It was not only a question of blood, rank and Royal Patronage, it was also that he was exceedingly wealthy.

His grandfather had married a great heiress and his mother had a dowry which exceeded that of any bride in the same year. He had inherited from her several houses and a large acreage of land in the north of England which grew more valuable year by year.

This combined with his father's family estate in Buckinghamshire and another in Leicestershire made Lord Kiniston one of the greatest Landlords in the whole of Great Britain.

He was well aware that this counted where Lillian was concerned, and he had often suspected that the many women who had desired him as a husband as well as a lover were thinking of his possessions as well as of himself as a man.

He therefore returned to his Château deciding that he must see Lady Charis immediately and inform her what was to be her future.

Although the Duke had promised him he would not speak of it, he could not help being afraid that he might inadvertently make Mrs. Patterson aware why he was unable to marry Elizabeth.

He was sure that the Duke must have talked it over with Marianne Patterson for she had obviously said that she favoured him as a brother-in-law.

Lord Kiniston did not underestimate Marianne's intelligence, and he was sure that if she guessed that he was to marry Lady Charis, or even if the Duke of Wellington swore her to secrecy, she would find it impossible to keep such an interesting piece of news to herself.

"What I have to do," he told himself in his usual efficient and decisive manner, "is to get officially engaged to Lady Charis. Then, if we find we are completely incompatible, we can in a few months declare that our engagement is at an end."

By then, he told himself, both Lillian and Elizabeth Caton would have disappeared from his life.

As he walked up the steps of his Château and the sentries came smartly to attention, Lord Kiniston looked closely at them just to make certain there was nothing about them with which he could find fault.

Then walking into the marble hall he saw the clock ticking in its marquetry case at the top of the stairs, and realised it was only nine o'clock.

He knew that Lillian would not be down for another two hours, and he suspected that after her tiring journey Lady Charis would also be late.

Nevertheless he asked the Major Domo:

"Is Lady Charis down yet?"

"Yes, indeed, M'Lord. She had breakfast half-an-hour ago, and is now, I think, in the stables looking at the horses."

Lord Kiniston raised his eye-brows.

"In which case I will go to find her."

Retracing his steps he walked out through the front door and towards the stables which were situated at the side of the house.

He saw the horse he had ridden being led through an arch which led into the cobbled yard, and as he followed it, he thought it unusual for any Society girl to rise so early or, for that matter, to be so interested in his horses.

The Caton sisters he knew rode well because they had been taught to do so since they could first crawl.

But they were not particularly interested in horses as horses, and Lillian only wanted an animal which would show off her attractions and make her friends envious.

Going to the stables, he found Alecia in a stall with one of his more obstreperous stallions.

He frowned when he saw where she was and said to the groom outside in the passage:

"Surely you warned Lady Charis that Hercules is sometimes dangerous?"

The groom looked embarrassed and said quickly:

"'Er Ladyship insisted Hercules wouldn't 'urt 'er, M'Lord, an' oi thinks she's roight."

Not wanting to startle the animal, Lord Kiniston stood still, looking through the railings into the stall.

Alecia had her back to him and he could see her fair hair silhouetted against the jet-black of the stallion's body.

She seemed very small and fragile beside such a large horse, but he realised as he listened that she was talking to the animal in a soft, caressing voice.

Hercules was obviously enjoying every moment of it and beginning to muzzle against her when she stopped stroking him.

"You are very, very beautiful," Lord Kiniston heard Alecia say, "as I expect you know, but it should make you proud, rather than conceited, and I am sure you could show all the other horses how to behave like real gentlemen."

She patted him again and turned away with a smile. Then she saw who was standing watching her.

She looked embarrassed as if she were a school-girl caught out doing something against the rules.

She came from the stall, bobbed Lord Kiniston a graceful little curtsy and said politely:

"Good morning, My Lord! I was getting acquainted with your magnificent horses."

"So I see!" Lord Kiniston remarked. "And you admire them?"

"I think they are wonderful! I have never seen such fine animals, and I am hoping you will allow me to ride them."

"But, of course!" Lord Kiniston said, "although I do not think your first mount should be Hercules."

Alecia looked disappointed before she said:

"I hoped you would allow me to ride him because, although your groom told me he could be very obstreperous, I know he would be good with me."

"How do you know that?" Lord Kiniston asked.

For a moment Alecia did not answer, and he said:

"I want to know why you say that."

"It is something I feel. As it happens, I prefer difficult horses to those that are too well behaved and what one might almost call goody-goodies."

She gave a little laugh as she spoke that had something childlike about it, and Lord Kiniston said:

"I am beginning to understand, Lady Charis, why you wish to set up a racing-stable."

For a moment Alecia wondered what he was talking about, then she remembered what Charis had said to her and how it was through her request to withdraw such a large sum that Lord Kiniston had become aware of her existence.

Because she was silent, Lord Kiniston thought she guessed that he intended to oppose the idea and he said quickly:

"Shall we go riding and afterwards have our talk?"

"I would love that!" Alecia exclaimed.

She hoped as they walked back towards the Château that their talk, whatever it might entail, would not last for long.

She changed quickly into her riding-habit and to her relief saw no one to ask questions as to what she was doing.

She had found when she came down to breakfast that none of the other guests in the house was present, and the servants informed her that Major Lygon had already breakfasted and left and that His Lordship was having breakfast with the Duke.

She had therefore eaten alone, and found it relaxing and, because there were so many delicious dishes to choose from, a delight she had not expected.

After the scanty meals she had been having at home

during the last few months, the dinner last night, which was more delicious than anything she had ever tasted, was a revelation.

So was the choice of half-a-dozen breakfast dishes, besides the newly-cooked *croissants*, and the first *fraises des bois* which the servants informed her were just becoming ripe.

She talked to them in French, and when they complimented her on her fluency she thought her mother would be proud that she was able to 'hold her own' in a foreign country.

It was when breakfast was over that she thought, rather than explore the downstairs rooms of the Château, which she could do at any time, she would be wise while she had the opportunity to go to the stables.

She had been sure Lord Kiniston would have some fine horses, but she had not expected them to be as outstanding as they were.

They were in fact far superior to those of her uncle, which she had been allowed to ride before he died.

Then she and her father had been left with only two old and second-rate animals, which they could not afford to replace with anything better.

When she reached the front door Lord Kiniston was already mounted on Hercules but waiting for her was an almost equally fine horse which was eager to be off.

They rode for an hour, and almost as if he was testing her Lord Kiniston set a sharp pace.

They galloped most of the time and it was impossible to talk until riding more slowly home Alecia said:

"That was wonderful! Thank you, thank you!"

"I am glad you enjoyed it," Lord Kiniston answered. "When you have changed, I will be waiting for you in my private study."

Alecia could not help thinking that one consolation at any rate of being here in her cousin's place was that she would have horses to ride which might have come out of her dreams.

She changed quickly and as she entered the room which Lord Kiniston considered his private sanctum, he was sitting at his desk.

As Alecia went in she saw there were some fine pictures by French artists on the walls and moved towards them with an exclamation of admiration.

"You like pictures?" Lord Kiniston asked.

"I love them," Alecia replied, "and Mama would have enjoyed this room as she would have enjoyed the rest of your Château."

As she spoke she remembered guiltily that she was talking about her own mother rather than Charis's.

In case she should make some obvious slip she turned to Lord Kiniston to say:

"Please, do not let us be too long talking. Having ridden one of your marvellous horses, who should all be called 'Pegasus', because they look fit for Greek gods or heroes to ride, I want to explore your Château."

Lord Kiniston laughed.

"You must tell them that, and I am sure, as you said to Hercules, it will make them proud rather than conceited."

To his surprise, Alecia blushed as if she felt she had been too effusive, and looked away from him shyly.

"Suppose we sit down?" Lord Kiniston suggested.

"Yes, of course," Alecia agreed.

She sat on the edge of a sofa which stood on one side of the fireplace, which as it was Summer was filled with flowers and pot-plants.

Lord Kiniston stood with his back to the mantelpiece and seemed for a moment, to be feeling for words before be said:

"I asked you to come to France, Lady Charis, because your father's Solicitors were not unnaturally surprised and somewhat perturbed by the amount of money you wished to invest in a racing-stable."

He paused, and as Alecia did not reply he went on:

"Now that I have seen your keen interest in horses I can understand that they attract you. At the same time, you will have to persuade me that the money will not be wasted."

He looked at Alecia piercingly as he said:

"Who suggested a racing-stable to you, and who is to be your partner in what could turn out a costly gamble?"

His question took Alecia by surprise, and she wondered frantically how she could answer it.

Charis had not prepared her for a cross-examination about the racing-stable and she had no idea what she should say.

She was therefore silent and after a moment Lord Kiniston said:

"I can only surmise, and of course, I will apologise if I am wrong, that some man you fancy has asked you to finance him in this ambitious project. Let me say immediately, it is something which, as your Guardian, I cannot allow!"

Alecia looked at him in a startled manner.

She was wondering frantically if his refusal to release the money could hurt Charis at the moment, or whether once she was married there would be nothing Lord Kiniston could do about it.

Then she remembered that he had asked her a question, and it was certainly untrue that Harry had asked Charis to finance him when he was himself rich and would be able to put the same amount of money as she did.

As she felt she must say something she murmured:

"It is not . . what you think."

"Nevertheless," Lord Kiniston said, "I cannot believe that a girl of your age intends to run a racing-stable on her own."

Alecia decided it would be wiser to say nothing, and she merely looked down so that her eye-lashes were dark against the whiteness of her skin.

As if her silence goaded Lord Kiniston into continuing what he was saying, he said after a moment:

"I have however a very different proposition to put before you, to which I hope you will listen carefully."

"I will . . try," Alecia murmured.

"You may suspect, in fact you must know, that a great number of the men who wish to marry you would not propose if it were not for the fact that you are endowed with such a large fortune," Lord Kiniston began. "It is, I imagine, very difficult for a young girl to differentiate between a man who is genuinely in love with her, and one who, while he may admire her, is more interested in her wealth."

"I . . do not believe that is true," Alecia said. "I think if a man was genuinely in love, one would know it, and in the same way one would . . be aware if he was . . pretending."

She was thinking of Harry Turnbury as she spoke, and how the look in his eyes and the tone of his voice when he spoke to Charis had told her beyond a shadow of a doubt that he loved her with his whole heart.

"My dear girl," Lord Kiniston said, "even much older and experienced women than you have been deceived. Without your father and mother to advise you, it is impossible for you to make the right sort of marriage to the right sort of man without their guiding hand."

"I think, My Lord," Alecia said softly, "that love .. true love .. which comes from the heart is something which cannot be .. enacted well enough to deceive .. anyone of any intelligence."

"That is your opinion," Lord Kiniston answered, "but not mine! I have therefore thought it over very carefully, and I have decided that for your own safety, and I am quite certain it would be your father's wish, that you should marry me!"

If a bomb had exploded at her feet, Alecia could not have been more surprised.

For a moment her body became still as if she was turned to stone. Then as she looked up at Lord Kiniston, her eyes seemed to fill her whole face.

"D.did you .. say .. " she stammered after a moment, "that I should .. m.marry *you*?"

"I am certainly no fortune-hunter," Lord Kiniston replied with a faint smile, "and I can offer you a position as my wife to which your father would have given his blessing."

"B.but .. but I do not .. love you!" Alecia stammered.

Lord Kiniston's lips twisted faintly in a smile before he replied:

"I think you will find, Lady Charis, that love between two people in the Social World, to which we both belong, comes after marriage. In France marriages are always arranged because the bride and bridegroom are suited both by blood and financially to one another. These alliances turn out most satisfactorily, and, as you well know, the same happens amongst most of the aristocratic families in England."

He paused before he continued:

"I therefore suggest that we announce our engagement, although of course there is no hurry for us actually to be married. We can have time to get to know each other first and feel sure that we are well suited, which I am convinced we will be."

"B.but . . I cannot . . marry you!" Alecia said desperately.

"Why not?"

"It is . . impossible! I cannot explain . . but of course such . . an engagement . . such an idea . . is impossible when . . we have . . only just met."

She was trying as she spoke to think of a reasonable argument which would convince Lord Kiniston that his idea was absurd, and in no circumstances would she agree.

But because her heart was thumping tempestuously in her breast, and because she was in fact, very frightened by what he had suggested, her head felt as if it was filled with cotton-wool, and it was impossible to think clearly.

"I gather you have had many proposals of marriage," Lord Kiniston said, "and you have refused them all. Why?"

That at any rate, Alecia thought, was an easy question to answer.

"Because I did not love the men who asked me to marry them."

"What you are saying, although you will not admit it," Lord Kiniston protested, "is that you knew they were not so much in love with you as bedazzled by your immense wealth, and of course, from a man's point of view, you are a very beautiful woman!"

"If I could not marry them because I did not love them," Alecia remarked, "then why should I . . marry you?"

She thought as she spoke that was rather clever, and Lord Kiniston did not miss the logic of it.

"For the reason I have already stated," he replied, "that I am quite convinced you are being pursued by fortune-hunters and bemused by their compliments and their flattery, and you may find yourself married to a man whose only interest in you is that you can swell his bank balance."

"I think that is not only cynical, but also a very unkind thing to say," Alecia remarked.

"Nevertheless, I am afraid it is the truth," Lord Kiniston insisted. "I am in fact, acquainted with some of the men who I understand have proposed to you, and may I say that I very much deprecate the fact, as I am sure your father would have, that your marriage has become a subject for bets in the Clubs of St. James's, and the members are already speculating as to which fortune-hunter will gain the 'golden prize' before the others."

"You make it sound . . horrid!" Alecia said, thinking of Charis and how deeply in love she was with Harry, and he with her.

"I am only being practical," Lord Kiniston said, "and therefore, however much you may protest, however much you may argue with me, Lady Charis, I intend to announce our engagement immediately!"

"But . . you cannot do that . . it is impossible . . !"

"Why?"

Alecia tried wildly to think of a reason why they

should not become engaged, but the only idea that came into her head was the truth, that she was not Lady Charis Langley, not the heiress, not the person they were betting about in St. James's.

"You see," Lord Kiniston said after a perceptible pause, "you really have no reason for refusing me, except that, as you say, you do not love me. I will therefore concede that if you are definitely not in love with me within six months, then we will terminate our engagement and inform the world that we made a mistake."

"You mean .. then I .. would not have to .. marry you?"

She felt as she spoke that she was grasping at a straw, trying to make some sense out of this frightening situation in which she felt as if she were swimming against a strong tide and making no headway.

"I promise you that I am a man of my word," Lord Kiniston replied. "If at the end of six months you ask to be released from an engagement which has become intolerable, perhaps to us both, I shall agree, and then we might think again about your idea of having a racing-stable of your own."

"I .. I suppose that would be .. all right," Alecia murmured.

At the same time she was worrying about how angry Lord Kiniston would be when he learned long before the six months came to an end that she was not Lady Charis, and Charis was in fact, already married to somebody else.

Again she clutched at a straw and tried to save herself.

"If .. if we are .. engaged," she said, "could we

please . . keep it secret . . entirely to ourselves . . so that no one . . will . . know?"

Lord Kiniston was however thinking of Lillian and Elizabeth.

"That would be a mistake," he said firmly. "After all, Charis, you are staying with me in my house which will inevitably give rise to a great deal of speculation. It is well known that I do not as a rule entertain young ladies here – in fact this is the very first time!"

"But . . if people did talk . . would it matter?" Alecia argued.

"What I am planning to do," Lord Kiniston said, "is to eliminate the fortune-hunters, especially the one who has asked you to provide him with £20,000 to be frittered away on horses that are not worth the price, or perhaps on other amusements of which you know nothing."

"How can you possibly know that that is what he would do?" Alecia demanded hotly.

"My dear child, I am considered a judge of men. In fact, the Great Duke himself often asks my advice. I therefore know very well the type of bounder who is prepared to sell his title and extort the highest price for it."

Alecia got to her feet.

"I think you have a very cynical and jaundiced view of people," she said, "and it is quite untrue."

"In your opinion!" Lord Kiniston replied. "As I have already said, you are far too young to know your own mind."

Alecia thought that Charis knew her own mind very well, and so did Harry, but how could she say so?

How could she convince Lord Kiniston that they were really in love?

In the meantime . .

She twisted her fingers together and in a very small voice she said:

"Please . . do not make me do this . . let me stay here for a few weeks then . . perhaps we could . . talk about it . . again."

She was thinking that by that time he would have learnt the truth.

Lord Kiniston shook his head.

"I cannot see any point in waiting," he said, "and I intend, Charis, whatever you may say, because I am your Guardian, and as your Guardian, I have your best interests at heart, to announce our engagement immediately.

"It will undoubtedly, as you are who you are, cause a sensation, but I am sure after all your success in London you will find that quite familiar, and extremely enjoyable."

He expected her to speak, and when she did not he went on:

"As I have already conceded, we will be engaged for exactly six months before we review the situation between us. After all, a broken engagement, as long as it is by mutual consent, will not hurt anybody, nor will it be the end of the world."

He spoke a little wryly, thinking that any other woman, especially Lillian and Elizabeth, would be rapturous at the idea of being married to him.

Instead Alecia only looked very pale, and he was aware, although he did not want to think about it, that her eyes were frightened and her fingers were trembling.

"It is wrong . . I know it is . . wrong!" she said. "And you . . have . . no right . . . .!"

"I have every right," Lord Kiniston interrupted,

"and if our engagement prevents you from receiving quite so many proposals of marriage, quite frankly that will do you no harm!"

He spoke contemptuously, and Alecia drew in her breath and to her own surprise she heard herself saying:

"I think you are behaving very badly, and if this is the way you trample over the French now that you have defeated them, then all I can say is that I am sorry for them . . very, very sorry . . indeed!"

Her voice broke on the last word and she turned and ran from the room, leaving Lord Kiniston staring after her in sheer astonishment.

CHAPTER FIVE

Alecia sat in her bedroom forcing herself not to burst into tears, as she wished to do.

She felt as if she had suddenly been drawn into a whirlpool and was being spun round and round until she could not think.

All she was conscious of was the dread that everything she might say or do would be wrong and Charis would suffer because of it.

She could not imagine what Charis would think when she read of her engagement to Lord Kiniston, unless she understood it was subterfuge forced upon her in order to play for time.

It was all so complicated and so frightening that Alecia could only sit with her hands over her face trembling until she realised it was nearly luncheon-time and it would seem strange if she did not appear.

She was frightened of the questions that those staying in the house would ask if Lord Kiniston told them of his engagement and she could only pray that he would not say anything for the moment.

If only he would wait, perhaps for a few days, by which time she might have fled to Paris and could escape home.

She was not quite certain how she could do that; for every conceivable means of extricating herself from an unpleasant situation seemed to flash through her mind, and almost before she could consider one, another took its place.

Finally she tidied her hair and thought when she looked in the mirror that she was extremely pale. Then she went slowly downstairs to the large Salon where she knew Lady Lillian and the other members of the house-party would be assembled.

To her relief Willy was there and he immediately came to her side to say:

"Good morning, Aphrodite! And let me tell you, you are looking more beautiful than you did yesterday!"

As she knew he was teasing her by using the nick-name by which Charis was known in London, she managed a brief little smile.

Then as she and Willy walked together to join the others Lady Lillian said with a sharp note in her voice:

"I understand, Lady Charis, that you have been out riding this morning! As I am your hostess, it would have been polite to let me know where you were going."

"I am so sorry," Alecia answered humbly, "but you had not been called and I did not like to disturb you."

"You would not have disturbed me," Lady Lillian replied disagreeably, "except that I would have cautioned you about risking your reputation as a young and unmarried girl by riding alone and unchaperoned."

As it had never struck Alecia for a moment that she should have been chaperoned, she could only look at Lady Lillian in surprise.

Before she could defend herself Willy said:

"Really, Lady Lillian, I think the conventions of Rotten Row are unnecessary here in Cambrai, and you can be sure that anywhere His Lordship and Lady

Charis went, they were not alone, but watched by hundreds of curious and, of course, admiring eyes."

Lady Lillian gave him a sour look, but before she could say anything Mrs. Belton came into the room greeting everybody effusively and telling anyone who would listen to her what a good night she had had.

"Such comfortable beds, dear Lady Lillian," she gushed. "I can assure you to lie on the one you have given me is like floating on the clouds!"

"You must congratulate the owner of the Château," Lady Lillian said as the *Duc* de St. Briere was announced. "I am sure he will appreciate how pleasant you find his home."

The *Duc* looking very elegant and un-English, kissed Lady Lillian's hand, and said something to her in a low voice which obviously pleased her. Then he went round greeting every woman in the room until he reached Alecia when he said:

"I admired you, Lady Charis, when I saw you in London at a Ball at Devonshire House. Now, you are even lovelier than I remember, and I am very honoured that my house should be a background for such beauty."

Because Alecia was embarrassed by the compliment she blushed a little and was looking extremely shy as Lord Kiniston came into the room.

He said 'good-morning' to some of the guests and holding out his hand to the *Duc* said:

"I am delighted to see you, St. Briere. I hope you do not find it disconcerting to have so many strangers invading your Château."

"On the contrary," the *Duc* replied, "I am exceedingly honoured that Your Lordship should be here. I only hope that you have been supplied with everything you desire."

93

"I have no complaints," Lord Kiniston smiled, "and now that you are in the neighbourhood, I hope I may have the pleasure of entertaining you, whenever you have no other engagements."

"Your Lordship is extremely gracious," the *Duc* said.

He spoke with what seemed complete sincerity, but watching the two men standing facing each other, Alecia suddenly had the strangest feeling that the *Duc* was, in fact, not as pleased with his tenants as he pretended.

She did not know why she should think such a thing, and yet as she watched him she thought that, while his lips smiled, his eyes were hard.

However, no one could have been more jocular or more amusing than the *Duc* at luncheon.

There were ten people present, and yet he managed to hold the table with his anecdotes and his condemnation of Bonaparte and everything he had done to France.

"A monster who has destroyed our young men and left the country so impoverished that it will take at least a generation to put it right!"

"I can understand your feelings, St. Briere," Lord Kiniston said, "but before we become gloomy and depressed, may I give you some cheering news of my own?"

There was silence as he spoke and everybody looked expectantly towards him as he sat at the head of the table. Then he said:

"I want you to congratulate me on being a particularly lucky man. I have today persuaded the beautiful Lady Charis to become my wife!"

For a moment there was a stunned silence, then Alecia saw an expression of fury in Lady Lillian's eyes.

Willy stepped quickly into the breach, and rising to

his feet and holding his glass high in his hand, said:

"Bravo, Drogo! Even though you have 'pipped me at the post', I can only congratulate you whole-heartedly! And to you, Lady Charis, my good wishes, and may you both be ecstatically happy to the end of your lives."

Because he was standing, everybody else with the exception of Lady Lillian rose to their feet and toasted Lord Kiniston and Alecia.

Because she felt deeply embarrassed and very shy, Alecia could only sit with a fixed smile on her face hoping that once the toasts were over she would be obliged to say as little as possible.

Then as they all sat down again the guests' voices rose in a kind of crescendo declaring how surprised they were, how they had no idea Lord Kiniston knew Lady Charis before she arrived, and of course asking how soon the wedding would take place.

This was a pertinent question and to Alecia's relief she heard Lord Kiniston reply:

"Unfortunately, we are unable to hurry over that. Charis wishes to be married in London, but it will be impossible for me to get away from here for some months, especially as the Duke of Wellington is talking of going to Cheltenham for a rest, and at the same time to have discussions with the Cabinet over the number of troops we should have in the Army of Occupation."

This started the inevitable arguments, which Alecia had already heard before, as to whether such a large Army was really necessary – and if in fact the Russians were a menace or not.

Alecia noticed that the *Duc* took little part in these discussions in which Major Belton and a Colonel, whose wife was also staying in the house, became very heated.

She found herself wondering what the *Duc* really felt about his Château and his country being occupied by foreigners, and whether, though he had helped the British against Napoleon, he resented their now having so much authority in his native land.

Watching him, she thought that when he looked at Lord Kiniston his features seemed to sharpen, and when the luncheon was over he went to Lady Lillian's side and began to flirt with her in what seemed to Alecia an almost outrageous manner.

She told herself it must be because she had seen so few sophisticated Society beauties in Little Langley that she thought her behaviour with the *Duc* was somewhat immodest and would certainly have shocked her mother.

It appeared as if, while the *Duc* was making advances to Lady Lillian, she was in her turn inciting them and flirting with him in a manner that seemed remarkably bold and unladylike.

Lord Kiniston of course was well aware how furious Lady Lillian was at the announcement of his engagement.

He understood exactly that by flirting with the Frenchman she was telling him in no uncertain language that there were other men in the world besides himself.

At the same time he did not underestimate her feelings for him, and he knew that sooner or later he would have to face an unpleasant scene although he hoped to avoid it.

In order to put it off for as long as possible he left the house as soon as he could, saying that he was wanted at the Barracks and the Duke was expecting him.

Once he had gone the rest of the house-party also disappeared, some to write letters.

Alecia was sure Mrs. Belton was hastening to write to her friends in England, describing her journey and without doubt Lord Kiniston's engagement to Lady Charis.

When she left the Salon Lady Lillian was seated on the sofa with the *Duc* de St. Briere. He was holding one of her hands in both of his and they were talking together in low voices in a very intimate manner.

She was not quite certain what she should do with herself and went to a room where she had seen a lot of books and beyond it she walked into a large Conservatory which had been built at a later date onto the side of the house.

There were not many flowers to be seen, but there was a cage of small birds which she thought was very attractive.

As she stood looking at them she heard some strange voices below the floor and wondered what they could be.

Looking out through the glass she saw two men coming from beneath the Conservatory, and she guessed they had been attending to the heating which rose through iron grids in the floor.

It was something she had seen in England at her Uncle's house, and she knew that if the Conservatory contained any exotic, or what were called 'hot-house' plants, they needed to be kept at a high temperature, even in the summer.

The men slammed down the cover over the exit from which they had emerged, then talking together using a strange argot that Alecia found hard to understand, they walked away.

As they did so she heard one of the men say to the other:

"*Ce qui nous manque maintenant est le cosmétique.*"

She knew this meant: "All we need now is *le cosmétique*," but she could not understand what they meant by *le cosmétique* in this context, and she supposed it must be some slang expression with which of course, she was unfamiliar.

Then, as she looked once more at the birds and the flowers which in fact were not particularly impressive, she supposed the *Duc* had not had much time since Napoleon's defeat and his return to France to refurbish the Conservatory.

She went into the Salon next door where the books were to be found and had some difficulty in choosing from a large collection what she would really like to read.

When at last she had found two that she knew she would enjoy, she sat down in the window-seat against the shutter that was folded back. The long crimson velvet curtains, which were very ornately tasselled and braided, were like a screen between her and the rest of the room.

She had read several pages and was just becoming interested in the plot when she heard the door open, and two people came into the room.

Because she had no wish to be disturbed, she tucked in her legs, which she had stretched out on the cushioned seat, and hoped they would go away without seeing her.

Then she heard the *Duc* de St. Briere say in French to the Major Domo who she knew was in charge of the household:

"Has everything been arranged?"

"*Oui, Monsieur le Duc*, everything is exactly as you requested."

"*Bon*! Now I want to know His Lordship's plans for the next few days."

The Major Domo hesitated for a moment before he said:

"Tonight there is a small dinner-party. For tomorrow I have not yet given any orders about luncheon, but *Monsieur le Duc de* Wellington is coming to dinner."

"That is what I have heard," the *Duc* remarked. "It is a large party?"

"*Non, Monsieur*, just about twenty, I think."

"*Bon!*" the *Duc* said again. "*Merci*, Beauvais, for your help."

"It is for *la belle France, Monsieur!*"

The *Duc* did not reply and Alecia heard him go from the room with the Major Domo following him.

As the door shut behind them she gave a sigh of relief and returned to her reading.

Lord Kiniston returned at about five o'clock to the Château.

Going to his private room he had only just begun to read the pile of papers that were waiting for him on his desk when Lady Lillian came in.

She was looking extremely alluring and he was experienced enough with women to know that she had taken a great deal of trouble over her appearance.

He rose perfunctorily as she walked towards him, then sat down again to say:

"I am very busy, Lillian, as you can see."

"Not too busy to talk to me, Drogo!"

"Must we talk? There is very little for us to say."

"I have a great deal to say, but I will not, as you

suspect I will, berate you for your cruelty in not telling me of your intentions before you announced them in public."

To Lord Kiniston's surprise she spoke quite pleasantly, but he knew by the expression in her eyes which she could not disguise that she was keeping a tight control on herself and was deliberately not raising her voice, but keeping it low and dispassionate.

"I am relieved about that," Lord Kiniston answered, "and I hope, Lillian, you will be pleasant to my future wife."

"You know what I feel about her, without my saying so," Lady Lillian replied. "But the real question, is it not, Drogo dear, is what about us?"

"I can only thank you," Lord Kiniston said hastily, "for the happiness you have given me, and hope that you will be tactful enough to understand that you should leave here as soon as possible."

Lady Lillian sat down on a chair in front of the desk before she replied:

"I hardly think that solution is worthy of you, Drogo! You intend to be married – very well – I suppose you have a good reason for it, although I can hardly believe that an unfledged girl who is not long out of the School-Room will keep you amused for long. But you and I mean something to each other which cannot be obliterated by an announcement in 'The Gazette' or for that matter, an engagement-ring on another woman's finger."

Lord Kiniston drew in his breath. Then he said in a cold, austere voice which those who disliked him knew so well:

"If you are suggesting what I think you are, Lillian, all I can say is that my answer is 'No!', most definitely

'No!' If I am to be a married man, then I will behave with propriety and like a gentleman."

Lady Lillian threw back her head and laughed.

"Darling Drogo, do you really think such a puritanical existence will keep you amused for long? Have you already forgotten the fire we can engender in each other? The wild passion which made us forget everything but ourselves."

Lord Kiniston looked down at the papers in front of him as if for inspiration before he said:

"I think, Lillian, this conversation is in extremely bad taste! I have just announced my engagement and, although I appreciate this may have come as a shock, you know as well as I do that you have many admirers waiting for you in London and in Paris, and it would be impossible in the circumstances for you to remain here."

"Why?" Lady Lillian asked. "Do you think I will tell your smug little Bride-to-be the truth about us? After all, she will have to learn that you are not exactly what you appear – a man, but also a very attractive, ardent, irresistible lover!"

Lady Lillian deliberately softened her voice as she said the last word, but Lord Kiniston was scowling and after a moment he said:

"This conversation, Lillian, is getting us nowhere! I would like you to leave this Château tomorrow or the next day at the very latest."

Lady Lillian's eyes narrowed and after a moment he thought she was about to rage at him.

Then clasping her hands together she said:

"How can you be so cruel, so heartless to me, Drogo? If you will not marry me, I refuse, utterly and completely refuse, to be cut out of your life."

"Nevertheless, I am afraid that is something that has to happen," Lord Kiniston said.

"But why? Marriage is one thing, love is another, as you well know. Have you no idea how much you will miss me after I am no longer here?"

"I dare say I shall survive," Lord Kiniston said sarcastically, "but one thing is quite obvious, Lillian, that you cannot continue to stay here as my hostess at the same time as the girl I am to marry."

"Send her away!" Lady Lillian said. "Send her back to London. You can follow her sooner or later. In the meantime we shall be very happy as we have been before she came."

Lord Kiniston rose to his feet.

"I am sorry, Lillian," he said. "I can only repeat what I have already said, that you must leave at the very latest by Thursday."

Lady Lillian rose too, and moving slowly as if she invited him to notice her grace and the sensuous movements of her body she came round to his side of the desk to stand beside him.

"And if I refuse to go," she asked very softly, "what will you do then?"

"It would be regrettable and might cause a lot of gossip," Lord Kiniston replied, "but I would take Lady Charis to Paris and find some distinguished and respectable chaperon for her, then spend as much time with her as is possible."

"But you could come back here to me?"

He shook his head.

"If you imagine I would do that you are mistaken. If I have to return I will stay with the Duke, who can always find room for me in his Château."

The way he spoke was quiet and calm, yet there was

an obvious steel in his words which made Lady Lillian know that she had lost the battle.

It was then, so quickly that she took him off his guard, that she flung herself at him, putting her arms around his neck and pulling his face down to hers.

"I love you! Oh, Drogo, I love you!" she cried, and pressed her body closely against his so that he could feel her warmth.

But before she could succeed in kissing him, Lord Kiniston firmly removed her arms from around his neck and pushed her away from him.

"Behave yourself, Lillian!" he said. "I have told you, I hope politely, that I am grateful for the happiness you have given me. Do not spoil it by making a quite unnecessary, and what would be for both of us, unpleasant scene."

For a moment Lady Lillian just glared at him, and it struck him that she was like a wild animal deprived of its prey.

Then without another word, she turned and walked from the room, slamming the door noisily behind her.

For a moment Lord Kiniston stood where she had left him, then as he sat down again at the desk he felt that he had been through a traumatic experience and yet, surprisingly, the roof had not fallen in on him.

For the moment he had escaped the tears and abuse that so often had terminated his love-affairs.

"Dammit all," he told himself, "it is time I was properly married, and preserved from enduring this sort of thing again!"

At the same time, he could not help being apprehensive that Lillian might not obey him and would refuse to leave the Château whatever he said to her about it.

Lady Lillian had in fact left him with a feeling of anger that contorted her face and made her feel as if a thousand knives were churning their way into her breast.

She had been so completely confident that Lord Kiniston would finally succumb to her blandishments and marry her as she wished him to do, that she could hardly believe he had become engaged to another woman, and at the same time thrown her out of his life.

"I will kill him!" she told herself as she walked up the stairs.

Then, just before she reached her own bedroom, she saw Alecia coming out of hers.

Alecia had in fact gone upstairs to tidy herself before tea. She knew it was something that was not served in a French household, but which the English ladies staying with Lord Kiniston would expect.

As Lady Lillian saw Alecia, her anger flared, and moving quickly towards her she said;

"I wish to speak to you, Lady Charis!"

"Yes, of course," Alecia replied.

She thought Lady Lillian would expect her to go with her but the elder woman pushed past her into her bedroom.

Then as Alecia followed her she said:

"I suppose you are aware that in becoming engaged to Drogo Kiniston you are stealing him from me and that he is behaving in an outrageous manner? I believed he would marry me!"

Alecia's eyes widened, but she was frightened by the way in which Lady Lillian was speaking and also by the hatred and fury she could see in her eyes.

"I . . I am sorry," she said after a moment, "if you are upset."

"Upset? What do you expect?" Lady Lillian demanded. "His Lordship has been my lover since the beginning of the year! Does that shock and surprise you? Yes? Well, listen to the truth for once, instead of living in some juvenile 'Cloud Cuckoo Land'. He loved me, he is mine, and you have no right to take him from me!"

Her voice as she said the last word, sounded like a snarl, and Alecia looking at her wondered how Charis would cope with such a situation and what she should say.

She was aware that if she were in love with Lord Kiniston and really wanted to marry him it would have been a terrible blow to have a woman like Lady Lillian saying such things to her and would in fact have made her very unhappy.

First of all she wanted to tell Lady Lillian that as far as she was concerned she could marry Lord Kiniston and it would not perturb her in the slightest.

At the same time she knew that Lady Lillian was a bad woman, and both her mother and her father would have been extremely shocked at her behaviour.

Although Lady Lillian was the daughter of a Duke she was certainly not behaving as a lady should.

"Well, what are you going to do about it?" Lady Lillian asked.

"What do you expect me to do?"

"It is quite obvious, unless you are half-witted, that you should refuse to marry him, and tell him to find somebody of his own age who understands what a man like him wants in a woman, which is certainly not a soppy milk-and-water unfledged girl!"

She seemed to spit the last words and Alecia said after a moment:

"I . . I am sorry, Lady Lillian. Of course I will speak to Lord Kiniston and ask him if he prefers to marry you, in which case I will naturally set him free."

She felt as she spoke that she had been rather clever, and she knew that her reply surprised Lady Lillian.

As if she found Alecia's behaviour a little bewildering, Lady Lillian screeched at her:

"Why do you not go back to where you have come from? Why have you come here upsetting everything, and persuading Drogo Kiniston to marry you when he has often sworn he would never marry? What hold have you over him? Can it be possible you are blackmailing him?"

The words seemed to spill out of Lady Lillian's crimson lips and almost as if she threatened her with physical violence, Alecia took a step back.

"I am sorry, Lady Lillian," she said again, "but I do not think I can help you. You must talk to Lord Kiniston, and of course I can only say that I will do anything he asks me to do."

As she finished speaking she turned, opened her bedroom door and went into the passage.

She thought she heard Lady Lillian murmur something, but she was not certain what it was.

All she wanted was to escape; to get away from a woman who she knew was immoral, if not evil, and have nothing more to do with her.

Because she was frightened, even though she had managed to keep her head and behave calmly, she ran down the stairs very quickly.

As she reached the hall she ran across it, but before

she could reach the door into the Salon she suddenly bumped into Lord Kiniston.

He put out his hands to steady her, then as she looked up at him, he saw the expression in her eyes and knew that something had upset her.

"What is the matter?" he asked. "What has occurred?"

Alecia was so out of breath that she could not answer him for a moment, and Lord Kiniston took her hand in his and drew her back down the passage to the room he had just left.

She did not protest. She was only struggling to get over her feelings of disgust at Lady Lillian's behaviour, and also, although it seemed stupid, she was afraid.

Still holding her hand Lord Kiniston drew her to the sofa and as she sat down on it he lowered himself beside her.

"Now, what has happened to make you look like that?" he asked gently. "Can it be that Lady Lillian has upset you?"

Because it was impossible for her to speak, Alecia merely nodded her head.

"I am sorry about that," he said. "She was very angry with me when she left me here a few minutes ago, and I suppose she had to vent her anger on somebody, and you were the first person she met."

"She . . she wants you to . . marry her," Alecia managed to say in a small voice.

"I know that," Lord Kiniston said, "but I have no intention of marrying Lady Lillian, or anyone else — except yourself!"

Having released her hand, Alecia clasped her fingers together and said, still in a small, frightened voice:

"She said how much more suitable . . she would be

for .. you than I could be, and .. I am sure she is right."

It flashed through Alecia's mind that while she had been frightened by Lady Lillian's violence and the things she had said, what was actually true was that she would make Lord Kiniston a far more suitable wife than somebody like Charis.

Her cousin wanted, like herself, the idealist love that had made Alecia's mother run away with her father.

"I wonder if I can explain this to you," Lord Kiniston was saying in a quiet voice that made him seem far less awe-inspiring than he usually was.

"Explain .. what?" Alecia enquired.

"The difference between the women in a man's life," Lord Kiniston replied.

Because, despite what she was feeling, this sounded rather interesting, Alecia looked at him for a brief second, then away again as he went on:

"The first woman a man loves is of course his mother, and if she is the right sort of mother she inspires in him a desire to find as his wife somebody like her, who will not only be kind, gentle and understanding, but also a guide and an inspiration, bringing out all that is best in him."

Because what he said sounded like a description of her own mother, Alecia looked at him again.

Although she did not speak he knew that she was listening intently.

"Then when he gets older," Lord Kiniston went on, "there are women who come into a man's life, whom he admires for their beauty, and finds them extremely pleasurable. But they are only a passing episode, and he has no intention of living with them on a perma-nent basis."

Alecia turned her head a little away from him, and because he felt she was shocked by what he was saying he continued very gently:

"These women are like flowers, beautiful as they come into bloom; but when they die, one throws them away because they are no longer attractive."

"They .. may not .. want to be .. thrown away," Alecia murmured.

"That is of course inevitable in some cases," Lord Kiniston replied. "At the same time, when a woman is older and perhaps a widow, there is no reason why she should not enjoy an interlude in her life which as a rule she has no desire to perpetuate any more than the man does with whom she has shared a few weeks or perhaps a few months."

"But .. surely .. it is wrong?"

"Not really," Lord Kiniston replied. "Life is short, and if people can find happiness, even if only for a short time, then they should be grateful. Men and women were created to be attracted to each other, but they also have other interests, other objectives besides making love."

There was silence, then Alecia said:

"I .. I am trying to .. understand."

"There is no reason for you to do that," Lord Kiniston said, "and I have not quite finished."

She looked up at him again enquiringly and he said:

"Besides his mother and the women who give him pleasure, a man is always looking for the woman he wants as his wife and the mother of his children. When he is young and idealistic, he is quite sure he will find her, and though often he is disappointed, he still goes on looking."

"And when he .. finds her?" Alecia asked.

"Then they are married, and as in all the fairy tales, live happily ever after!"

Now there was a touch of cynicism in Lord Kiniston's voice, but Alecia did not notice it. Instead she said:

"I think I understand .. but perhaps .. because she loves you .. you would be happy if you .. married Lady Lillian."

"Do you really think," Lord Kiniston asked, "that she would be the right sort of mother for the son I hope one day will succeed me?"

As he spoke Alecia saw a quick picture of Lady Lillian's face as she had just seen it contorted with fury, and she also saw her flirting with the *Duc* de St. Briere, as she had at luncheon.

Behaving like that, she could not imagine her holding a baby in her arms, or giving it the love Lord Kiniston had received from his mother, and she had had from hers.

"I think I do .. understand," she said after a moment, "and thank you for .. explaining it to .. me."

"What I want," Lord Kiniston said, "is for you not to be upset by Lady Lillian, and I hope that she will leave here if not tomorrow, then the day after."

"I expect she would like to stay for the dinner you are giving for the Duke of Wellington."

"How do you know about that?"

"I happened to hear the Major Domo telling the *Duc* de St. Briere that he was expected."

For a moment Lord Kiniston frowned, as if he resented the idea of his gossiping. Then he said:

"Servants will talk, and there is nothing one can do to stop them. But now, Charis, I think you should come to have a cup of very English afternoon tea."

Alecia smiled.

"I must admit if I had to go without it I should miss it."

"Very well," Lord Kiniston said. "We will go to join the others, where I am quite certain they will be gossiping around the tea-pot!"

The way he spoke made Alecia laugh.

Then as they both rose and walked towards the door, she thought it was a very strange conversation to have with a man who had just announced his engagement to her without asking her permission, and who had, until this moment, seemed very frightening.

"He can be nice when he wants to be," she told herself as they walked down the passage side by side.

Then as he opened the door of the Salon she instinctively moved a little nearer to him, as if she was in need of protection.

Lord Kiniston appeared to understand.

"It is all right," he said quietly. "I will look after you, and I promise you there is nothing to be frightened about! These are only people who are envious because they are not as beautiful as you, or as rich as me!"

He was speaking with a mocking note in his voice, and as he opened the Salon door, Alecia gave a little laugh.

CHAPTER SIX

There was a party of twelve at luncheon and the *Duc* was one of the guests.

Once again he paid tremendous court to Lady Lillian who seemed to Alecia to have recovered somewhat from her rage.

Although she spoke in a soft, sweet, rather hurt voice to Lord Kiniston, she once again deliberately flirted with the *Duc* hoping, Alecia was sure, to make him jealous.

Alecia was thankful that she was seated next to Willy who regaled her with stories of how difficult the French were being over the Army of Occupation.

He was convinced that only the Duke of Wellington's tact had managed to keep everything under control with no one becoming too angry with anyone else. And it was obvious that he was an ardent admirer of the Duke.

When luncheon was over, everybody dispersed.

Mrs. Belton and two other English ladies said they were going shopping and invited Alecia to go along with them.

Alecia refused. She was very conscious that all the money she had with her, and it was not very much, would be needed if she had to find her own way home to England in disgrace.

Charis had given her £15 for the journey, thinking it would be enough to tip the servants and for any small things she wanted.

Her ticket had been provided for her by Lord Kiniston and the Courier, Mr. Hunt, had held it in his possession for safe keeping.

She was quite certain there was no return ticket with it, and she was calculating how much she would need for a carriage and horses to take her to Calais, her ticket on the Packet across the Channel, and for the carriages on the other side.

It was difficult to know exactly what would be required, and she thought it would be a mistake to ask in case anyone was suspicious that she was thinking of returning to England.

Therefore she knew the last thing she must do was to dissipate her money on trivialities.

Mrs. Belton had already enthused over how attractive the materials and ribbons were in France, but she told herself she had to be strong-minded and anyway she had the beautiful clothes which Charis had given her.

When the other women had gone upstairs to put on their bonnets, and the men had disappeared in the direction of the Barracks, Alecia went into the Salon with a book she was in the middle of reading.

She had noticed that outside one of the long French windows of the Salon there was a delightful shaded place among the flowers where one could sit to read.

It was out of the sun, and with the shrubs in blossom scenting the air she thought it was very romantic.

When she found there was nothing there to sit on, she went back into the Salon, and picking up one of the cushions from a chair, brought it out and set it down just outside the open windows so that her back was against the wall of the Château.

She was very comfortable, and it was the way she often sat reading at home.

Now she liked looking out over the formal gardens which she knew had been designed in imitation of the exquisite gardens of Vaux le Vicomte which lay outside Paris.

She longed above anything else to see the City of which she had read so much and whose history had always enthralled her.

She found herself remembering how at luncheon someone had said to the *Duc* de St. Briere that it was extraordinary how the French had decided to celebrate the Fall of the Bastille every 14th July.

"Surely," Lady Lillian had said, "the one thing you, and most sensible Frenchmen, want to forget is the Revolution!"

"It is certainly something I do not wish to recall," the *Duc* agreed. "At the same time, the French love celebrations and every country has special days when they remember outstanding episodes in their history."

"That is true enough!" Louisa Caton, who was present with her *fiancé*, Colonel Felton-Hervey, exclaimed. "We celebrate the 4th July when we won our Independence from the English!"

"I feel we should have had a day of mourning to remember how we lost America," Colonel Felton-Hervey said, then added gallantly: "but I am doing my best to get one little bit of it back!"

Louisa pouted at him prettily and Lord Kiniston remarked:

"We have St. George's Day on which to celebrate the greatness of England, and perhaps in the future we will dedicate a day to the Battle of Waterloo."

There was a little murmur of appreciation at this

from the English present, but Alecia thought that the *Duc* took no part in it.

Because she considered it was a little tactless to draw attention to the way his country had been defeated, even though it was under the generalship of Napoleon Bonaparte, she said:

"We must not forget that we celebrate Guy Fawkes Day on 5th November when they unmasked the plot and saved Parliament."

"That is true," Lord Kiniston agreed, "but I think Guy Fawkes is remembered because he chose such an original way of silencing Parliament, which talked too much, then and now!"

Everybody laughed at this and the conversation became political.

There was an argument as to who was the most vociferous politician at Westminster, and whether Lord Kiniston, when he returned home, would be continually speaking in the House of Lords.

'I am sure he would make very good speeches,' Alecia thought.

She knew that, although he was intimidating, she could not help admiring the sharpness of his brain: he always seemed to have a new angle on every argument, and his opinions seemed to her shrewder and more convincing.

'I can understand why he has been such a success in his career,' she decided and could not stop her thoughts from returning to herself and wondering whether when Lord Kiniston knew the truth about her, he would be very, very angry.

She was deep in her thoughts when she heard voices through the open window above her head, and realised it was the *Duc* speaking.

115

"I wanted to say goodbye to you alone, before I left," he said.

"You are leaving?"

"Only for a few days," the *Duc* replied consolingly, "but I have to go to Paris to see my mother who is not well."

"I am sorry, but I shall miss you."

"Is that true, really true? There is no need for me to say how much I shall miss your beauty, and the sweetness of your voice."

"I shall be counting the days until you return," Lady Lillian said softly.

"And you know I shall do the same," he replied, "but I have a favour to ask of you before I go."

"What is it?"

"Tonight, at the dinner-party which, alas, I cannot attend, I have arranged for there to be a special present for the three people I admire most."

"It sounds exciting!" Lady Lillian exclaimed.

"I hope you will think so," the *Duc* said, "and I want you to promise me that although I shall not be here to see it happen, you will take the Duke of Wellington and Lord Kiniston into the Conservatory at exactly a quarter before ten."

"And what is going to happen when we get there?"

"It will be something special to commemorate the Duke's brilliant leadership at Waterloo, and similarly for Lord Kiniston. And for you, my divine lady, something which will make you remember me."

"How could I ever forget you?" Lady Lillian asked. "But I am very curious. Do tell me what it is."

"No, no, that would spoil everything," the *Duc* protested. "It all has to be a surprise. But I will give you a hint and say that your gift sparkles."

Lady Lillian gave a cry of delight.

"Oh, Flavian, do you mean . . are you really giving me that necklace I admired?"

"That you will have to find out for yourself," the *Duc* said mysteriously, "but I would not wish you to be disappointed. Do not forget your promise."

"Is it likely that I should do anything so stupid?" Lady Lillian asked. "I will have the Duke and Drogo in the Conservatory at a quarter to ten and the rest of the party must come too."

"Why not? They will be very welcome," the *Duc* replied.

"Must you really go? Can you not wait until to-morrow?"

"My mother is expecting me. Meantime I beg of you, as the most beautiful woman I have ever seen, to take care of yourself until I return, and not to forget me."

"How could you imagine for one moment I would do so?" Lady Lillian asked.

There was a little silence and Alecia thought, incredible though it seemed, the *Duc* was kissing Lady Lillian.

Then he said, his voice deep as velvet:

"You intoxicate me with your beauty, and I shall be thinking of you all the way to Paris."

"And I of you," Lady Lillian replied.

The *Duc* must have looked at the clock for he said:

"I must go! My horses are waiting."

"I will come to see you off."

There was a movement which told Alecia they were walking towards the door.

Then as she heard it shut behind them she heaved a sigh as if she released her breath, and knew she had been holding it without being aware of it.

How, she asked herself, after all Lady Lillian's protests of affection for Lord Kiniston, could she behave in such an outrageous manner with the *Duc* de St. Briere?

What was more, she was actually accepting what Alecia was sure was a very expensive present from him.

She had been brought up to believe that the only things a woman could accept from a man, unless she was his wife, or they were engaged to be married, were trivial presents like a fan, a pair of gloves, or a bottle of scent.

A necklace which sparkled could only be made of diamonds, and she was appalled that Lady Lillian should accept anything so valuable from a man, who, even if he was an aristocrat, was, owing to his nationality, an'enemy of Great Britain.

It was all very unpleasant, she thought, and it certainly seemed strange that the *Duc* wished to give the Duke of Wellington and Lord Kiniston presents as well.

She supposed they would be commemorative plaques or something of that sort.

At the same time, it seemed strange that he should wish to do so, even though Lord Kiniston had said that he had been useful to the English when he returned to his own country in disguise before the defeat of the Emperor Bonaparte.

'There is something about him I do not like,' Alecia thought to herself.

Then she told herself she was just prejudiced and, when the Duke of Wellington and Lord Kiniston both accepted him, who was she to find fault?

She opened her book, but found it difficult to concentrate on the written word when she had so many things to think about which were happening around her.

If she had not been so agitated and nervous at having to impersonate Charis, she would have enjoyed being in the centre of things at Cambrai.

Anyone in England would have been overwhelmed with excitement at meeting and being in close proximity with the hero of the day, and she knew as a quiet 'country bumpkin' it was something she would remember for the rest of her life.

'I must enjoy every minute of it,' she thought, 'because the moment Lord Kiniston learns that Charis is married and I am a fake, I shall be sent home in deep disgrace and it is doubtful if anybody will ever speak to me again!'

She knew too that when she listened to the conversation at the dinner-table, she was privileged as few people in England were to know what was happening in Paris.

She tried to understand the complexities of the Quadruple Alliance which had been proposed by Viscount Castlereagh, and which involved there being a permanent conference of four Ambassadors at Paris during the Occupation to keep an eye on France for any sign of a recurrence of Revolutionary spirit.

It certainly seemed to Alecia from the soldiers moving around in Cambrai that there was enough of the British Army there to prevent any Revolutionary uprising.

She was also sure the average French peasant was as sick of war as was everybody else.

Then she told herself that she was not in a position to judge, and because she was shy, she did not like to ask a great number of questions.

It struck her that if she could talk about it alone with Lord Kiniston, it would be very exciting, and something else which she would be able to remember.

When they were riding it was impossible to have a continuous conversation, and at other times there were always people about, especially Lady Lillian.

Now that she had had time to think it over, she

decided she disliked Lady Lillian intensely, and that she was in fact a wicked and evil woman.

There was something about her which was repellent, even though she was so beautiful.

Alecia wondered what Lord Kiniston really felt for Lady Lillian and if, although he had said he had no intention of marrying her, he would prefer to remain unmarried and enjoy himself with the women he had described as 'flowers' to be thrown away when they withered.

There did not seem very much that was withered about Lady Lillian, but if he had ever seen her in the same sort of rage as she had shown that morning to Alecia, she was certain that he would decide he would be wise to dispense with her.

"Besides," Alecia argued to herself, "how can any woman be so two-faced as to declare that she loves one man, yet flirt outrageously with and accept presents from another?"

It made her feel very young and lost.

Lord Kiniston had said he would look after her and there was nothing to be frightened about, but she knew she was frightened of Lady Lillian.

She was frightened by Lord Kiniston himself, and by the large number of people who kept coming and going in the Château.

She had a sudden longing to be back at home where, even though she felt lonely, there were the horses to ride and the quietness and solitude of the woods.

There she could feel that life was pulsating through everything, bringing strange music to her heart.

It was a feeling of happiness that was different from what she felt when people were chattering and laughing all around her.

It struck her that what would be most wonderful would be to find a man with whom she could share her feelings for the country and the animals which had always meant so much to her.

Then suddenly, almost like a blow, she could see Lord Kiniston's face in front of her.

Because what she was thinking made her cry out at the absurdity of it, she put her hands up to her face and forced herself to repudiate everything her heart was telling her.

A long time later, it seemed to Alecia, she heard the voice of Mrs. Belton talking animatedly in the Salon and realised the ladies had come back from their shopping expedition.

"What I am really longing for," Mrs. Belton said, "is a cup of tea. I cannot understand why the French always seem to prefer coffee, when I can think of nothing more reviving than tea."

"I agree with you," another lady said in English.

It was the sort of thing Alecia had heard them say before, and thinking it absurd to sit outside, listening to what they were saying, she decided to go in and join them.

She rose, realising as she did so that she had not read one page of the book which had been lying in her lap. She had instead been thinking thoughts that she wanted to forget, but was quite certain it would be impossible to do so.

Carrying her book and the cushion on which she had been sitting she went in through the open windows, and Mrs. Belton gave a cry of delight at seeing her.

"Oh, there you are, Lady Charis! I do wish you had

come with us! We have found the most exciting things and so cheap they were really almost given away."

"I think the French are thankful to have anything to sell after a war in which 'that monster', as the *Duc* called him," another of the ladies said, "sacrificed everything to the making of guns and ammunition."

"That is true," Mrs. Belton agreed. "At the same time we might as well benefit by what we can buy at such reasonable prices, and the shop-keepers seemed extremely pleased to see us."

"I wonder what the French really feel about us?" another Englishwoman asked.

Mrs. Belton laughed.

"I think it would be a mistake to probe too deeply. As far as I am concerned, as long as they are polite, and no longer wish to kill my husband, I am quite content to enjoy myself in France, and I am looking forward to the chance of visiting Paris."

"So am I!" both the other women present exclaimed.

Then the talk was only of the gaieties that were taking place in Paris every night, and they were all extremely envious that they could not participate in them.

"I suppose you know," Mrs. Belton said with the air of somebody who has information no one else has, "that the Duke is planning a great Ball in June, before he leaves for England."

There was a cry of excitement as both the other ladies said:

"No, we were not told about it."

"He is giving it in honour of the Royal Princes in his mansion in the Champs Élysées."

"How exciting!" one of the ladies exclaimed. "Will we all be able to go?"

Anyone in England would have been overwhelmed

"My husband thinks we will be invited," Mrs. Belton replied. "You know how His Grace always wants 'his boys' as he calls them, to enjoy the same things as he does."

"Why did you not tell us before?" one of the ladies said. "You know we will all have to get new gowns."

"Yes, that is true," Mrs. Belton agreed, "but whatever we do, Lady Charis will be the Belle of the Ball and there is no use our trying to compete with her."

She smiled kindly at Alecia as she spoke, who looked embarrassed.

Then as the door opened for the servants to bring in tea, Mrs. Belton said in a conspiratorial tone:

"But not a word to anyone! The Ball is a secret until the Great Man tells us about it himself."

"Yes, of course, we will be very discreet."

As they went up to dress for dinner, Alecia thought it was very unlikely that she would be present at the Ball in Paris, since by that time Charis's wedding would have taken place.

She supposed she would hear from her that the charade was over and she could resume being herself and go back to England.

Then, as she was lying in her bath, she knew that she did not want to go back to England as urgently as she had in the first moments of her arrival, and again this afternoon.

What she wanted was to stay a little longer with Lord Kiniston; to listen to him talking, and to enjoy – for it would be very stupid of her not to – the strange but exciting life here that was different from anything she had ever known before.

"I am very, very lucky," she told herself. "What other girl would have such a chance after living so quietly and inconspicuously at Little Langley with no one to talk to except for Papa, who does not listen, and old Bessie, whose mind is always on food?"

She was glad to think that when she did return her father would be well fed for a long time on the money which Charis had given them.

Then inevitably her mind went to the delicious dishes she was enjoying in the Château cooked by a French Chef, who Lord Kiniston had said casually at luncheon was, in his opinion, better than the one employed by the Duke of Wellington.

"You will certainly have to make sure," Willy said, "that Alfonse excels himself tonight, so that you make the Great Man envious."

"The trouble is," Lord Kiniston replied, "that as Mrs. Patterson is coming with him, I feel his mind will not be on the food!"

Everyone laughed at that and Willy said:

"I should not be too sure. After all, his admiration for Mrs. Patterson only shows his good taste, and the French manage to make food an art, rather than a necessity."

They all laughed again and Alecia thought that before she left she must try to learn the recipes of some of the French dishes so that now they could afford the more expensive ingredients she could make them for her father.

When she had finished her bath Sarah helped her into one of the pretty gowns Charis had given her which she had not worn before.

The pale pink of a musk rose, it was decorated round the hem and sleeves with tiny roses, and the ribbons which crossed over her breasts and hung down her back were of silver.

"You do look pretty, M'Lady, you do, really!" Sarah exclaimed. "An' I've persuaded them gardeners, though it was difficult to make 'em understand, to give me some roses for to put in your hair."

"That was kind of you, Sarah," Alecia said. "Are you learning to speak French?"

"A word or two, M'Lady, but from what I hears, all them Frenchies want to talk about is what they calls '*l'amour*'!"

Alecia laughed.

"I should listen to their compliments, Sarah. It will be something to remember when you get back, for Englishmen do not say half such nice things!"

"That's true, M'Lady," Sarah agreed, "though my English boy-friend manages all right when I pushes him!"

That was true of all Englishmen, Alecia thought.

She went down the stairs thinking of the effusive compliments which the *Duc* de St. Briere paid in language which seemed to her not really sincere.

She knew it was not the way she would want the man with whom she was in love to speak to her.

As she entered the Salon she realised that because the Duke of Wellington was coming to dinner, all the women present were wearing their best gowns and Lady Lillian was glittering like a Christmas-tree in a dress covered in sequins.

She was also wearing an exquisite emerald necklace while round her wrists were matching bracelets, and she wore a small tiara of the same stones on her dark hair.

She looked spectacular.

At the same time, Alecia thought, rather like the

witch in a fairy-tale who was intent on ensnaring the Knight who had come to slay the dragon.

Then she rebuked herself for being uncharitable.

The expression she saw in Lady Lillian's eyes however told her that the older woman positively loathed her.

Her animosity seemed to vibrate from her so strongly that instinctively Alecia went to the other side of the room to avoid her.

Soon the Duke of Wellington arrived, and on meeting him Alecia was aware that he had indeed an aura of magic and leadership about him.

She had always imagined a great man would have it, and she felt it vibrate from him in an unmistakable manner.

She knew that even if she had been blind and the Duke had come into the room, she would have been aware that it was him.

She was introduced to him by Lord Kiniston and the Duke said:

"Now that I see you, Lady Charis, I can understand how so many young men have been bowled over by your beauty. But you have taken from me my most indispensable General."

"I have no intention of doing that, My Lord," Alecia managed to reply.

"Until you came into his life," the Duke said, "I believed him to be wholeheartedly a soldier. Now I am suspicious about which direction he will be looking, and I have a feeling it will be yours."

He spoke in a clipped, but slightly humorous manner which did not make a compliment seem embarrassing or make Alecia feel shy.

Instead she smiled and said:

"I can still hardly believe that I am privileged enough to meet Your Grace."

"This, I hope, is the first of many meetings," the Duke answered gallantly.

As he turned away to speak to somebody else Alecia knew Lord Kiniston was pleased by the way she had behaved.

She had an impulse to slip her hand into his and say that she had been afraid she might let him down, and that the Great Man might ask why he should want to marry her.

Then she told herself that the person who would really be most horrified if he knew the truth was the Duke of Wellington.

In her sudden feeling of fear she was not aware that Lord Kiniston was watching the expression in her eyes, and he said to her in a quiet voice that no one else could hear:

"What is worrying you? I want you to enjoy yourself, Charis. This is a very special evening."

"Yes, I know," Alecia replied, "and it is .. very exciting to meet the Duke."

"Then do not look so worried about it! I can assure you he is a great admirer of yours."

Alecia managed to smile back at him. Then other guests began to arrive, and by the time everybody was introduced and had had a glass of champagne dinner was announced.

Because Lady Lillian was still acting as hostess, the Duke was seated on her right and Alecia was on his other side.

It was very clear from the start that Lady Lillian had no intention of allowing Alecia to speak to the Duke if she could help it, and she monopolised him with an expertise that came from years of enchanting men with her beauty and her wit.

Alecia gave up the struggle to talk to the Duke as she would have liked to do, and contented herself with chatting to Willy who was on her other side.

This meant she could also watch Lord Kiniston where he was seated at the head of the table next to the attractive Mrs. Patterson.

Both her sisters were also dining at the Château that night, and Alecia could understand why they were called 'The Three Graces'. Certainly it was obvious that both the Duke and Colonel Felton-Hervey found them irresistible.

When the ladies left the gentlemen to their port, Alecia had the feeling that Lady Lillian was going to be offensive to her, so to avoid coming in contact with her she hurried up the stairs to her bedroom.

She thought perhaps she was being over-sensitive.

At the same time, she knew it would be embarrassing if Lady Lillian decided to show off to the Caton sisters and to the other guests her animosity for Lord Kiniston's fiancée.

Mrs. Patterson had already given her her good wishes and so had Louisa, who was engaged to Colonel Felton-Hervey.

Elizabeth on the other hand had been cold and distant and it suddenly occurred to Alecia that perhaps she had wanted to marry Lord Kiniston, and was annoyed that he had chosen a different bride.

It was only an idea, but she thought it would be uncomfortable for her to talk to the ladies in the Salon until the gentlemen joined them.

Having therefore gone up to her bedroom and tidied her hair and put just a suspicion of powder on her small nose as Charis had directed her to do, she went to the window and drew back the curtain to look out.

The garden was full of shadows and although it was growing dark, there was just the remains of a crimson and gold sunset vanishing behind the tall poplar trees.

It was very beautiful and Alecia knew that instead of chattering downstairs she would much prefer to walk in the garden, with perhaps one person beside her to enjoy the beauty of the night.

As she stood at the window she saw a movement towards the far end of the Château and wondered what it could be.

Then she saw two men approaching what she knew was the Conservatory, and remembered how she had seen them the previous day and thought they must be stoking the boilers.

She supposed they were doing the same thing now, then thought it strange that they should still be on duty at this time of the night, although doubtless the French worked different hours from the British.

The men disappeared and then another man appeared out of the shadows moving in the same direction.

He was wearing a dark cloak and he looked different from the two previous men who were obviously workmen.

He walked hurriedly and there was something about him which seemed to Alecia vaguely familiar.

Then she thought, although of course it must be impossible, that he had the same figure and was the same height as the *Duc*.

She told herself that perhaps all Frenchmen looked very much alike, and the *Duc* by this time would be well on his way to Paris to see his sick mother.

The man in the cloak disappeared – under the Conservatory, she supposed, like the workmen.

A few minutes later, after she had looked up at the sky and searched for the first evening star twinkling in the encroaching night, she was aware that the men she had seen were leaving.

The man in the cloak appeared first. Now he was moving very much more quickly than when she had first seen him.

In fact, he appeared to be almost running, and there was something almost furtive about his behaviour.

The two workmen were not in such a hurry, but Alecia realised that their arms were empty whereas before they had been carrying something heavy.

'I hope it is not too hot in the Conservatory,' she thought, 'for it is a warm night, and if the Duke and Lord Kiniston are to receive their presentations there, they may feel it obligatory to make short speeches of thanks, even though the *Duc* is not there.'

Then she realised she must go downstairs because they had lingered over dinner and it would soon be the time appointed by the *Duc* for them to be in the Conservatory.

In fact, when she came downstairs the men appeared in the passage which led from the Dining-Room and were entering the Salon.

They were received by Lady Lillian who said:

"Before you sit down, Gentlemen, I have a little surprise for His Grace and for our charming host in the Conservatory."

"A surprise!" Lord Kiniston exclaimed. "What is it?"

"You will see when you get there," Lady Lillian replied, "and I promised that we would be in the Conservatory on the stroke of a quarter to ten."

"It sounds intriguing," the Duke said, "and of course Lady Lillian, we must not disrupt your plans!"

As Alecia joined them she realised that Lord Kiniston was frowning, as if he did not like to be confronted with surprises in what was, to all intents and purposes, his own house.

It was some distance to the Conservatory at the other end of the house, and she found herself walking beside him and Willy, while the Duke and Lady Lillian led the way and the rest of the party followed.

When they reached the Conservatory for a moment Alecia could not see that it looked very different from the way it had the day before.

Then she realised it had been lit by candles put discreetly behind the flowers at the far end of it, to which they had to walk right across the Conservatory to reach three objects covered by cloths.

One was of gold, one of silver, and the third was smaller and green, which told Alecia that that covered the present for Lady Lillian.

Then as she looked, thinking that after all the Conservatory did not seem very hot, for which she was thankful, she remembered what she had heard one of the men say to the other as they left the Conservatory the day before.

"All we need now is '*le cosmétique*'!" he had remarked.

Suddenly she remembered, as if strangely prompted by some Fate, that the word *cosmétique* could include powder in its meaning, and that conceivably it might be criminals' slang for gun-powder.

Instantaneously, as if her eyes were suddenly opened, she knew what was going to happen.

It was the *Duc* she had seen, and what the other two men had been carrying was gun-powder with which to

131

blow up the Conservatory and with it the Duke of Wellington and Lord Kiniston, together with everybody else there.

By this time the Duke and Lady Lillian were moving towards the three objects elegantly surrounded by flowers.

Alecia gave a shrill scream that seemed to pierce the air and make it echo all around the walls of glass.

"It is a plot .. a plot!" she screamed. "We are going to be blown up! Run .. run out of here as quickly as you can!"

Her words seemed to fall over themselves, but as the Duke and Lady Lillian turned to stare at her in astonishment Lord Kiniston acted.

He rushed to the side of the Conservatory where he kicked open a glass door which had been closed.

As he did so, the Duke, as if he also was used to emergencies, pulled Lady Lillian out into the garden, and Alecia felt Lord Kiniston's hand grasp her wrist.

He dragged her roughly through the door and some of the other guests hastily followed.

"The place is about to explode!" Lord Kiniston shouted. "Hurry! Hurry! There is no time to think, just get out as quickly as you can!"

As he spoke, the stragglers at the back who had only just reached the entrance to the Conservatory from the house, were pushed back by Willy.

Because the three men were so quick in their movements and reacting to what Alecia had said, the Conservatory was almost instantaneously emptied, and the Duke of Wellington was now standing with some others in the garden looking back at the glass building speculatively.

Alecia of course now began to fear that perhaps

she had been mistaken, and thought how foolish she would feel if nothing happened and the men she had seen were genuine workmen, occupied simply in stoking the fires.

Then there was a slight rumble and as it came Lord Kiniston pushed her violently down on the grass and flung himself on top of her.

For a moment, because his action was so surprising, her breath was knocked out of her body.

Then as she felt the heaviness of him cover her, there was a tremendous bang followed by two other minor explosions, and a crash of glass that seemed to shatter the quietness of the whole world and ring in her ears long after it was finished.

As she grasped the fact that she had been right in her suspicions, she looked up and found Lord Kiniston's face very near to hers.

She was conscious of how heavy he was, and how small and helpless she felt beneath the strength of his body.

Then as she looked up at him, frightened by what had happened, and yet at the same time aware that everyone had been saved, above all, Lord Kiniston himself, he said very quietly:

"Thank you, Charis! You have saved us all!"

As he finished speaking, his lips came down on hers.

For a moment she could hardly believe it was happening.

Then as he kissed her she knew that the only thing that mattered to her was that she had saved him.

CHAPTER SEVEN

Lord Kiniston released Alecia's lips and, moving himself carefully off her body, stood up.

As he did so Alecia was aware of what was happening around them.

Women were screaming shrilly, the sound mingling with the crackling flames of the fire which was now rapidly consuming the Conservatory.

There were huge sparks flying up into the air, which made those nearest to the wreckage scramble away from it as quickly as they could.

The Duke, who had also flung himself on the ground and made Lady Lillian do the same, was now on his feet and like Lord Kiniston was looking around to see if anyone was injured.

A spark had set alight Elizabeth Caton's muslin gown, but Colonel Felton-Hervey had beaten it out.

He himself had been struck by a splinter of burning wood on his forehead, which had left a crimson mark.

Another of the guests had a burning ember caught in her hair, and it was she whom Alecia had heard screaming until she was rescued by two male members of the party.

It was all very confusing and for a moment it was difficult to think. Then, as if he knew it was for him to take command, the Duke said:

"Will everybody go into the Salon where we met for dinner."

As they moved across the garden towards the further end of the Château, Alecia deliberately did not look back at the burning Conservatory.

She could not bear to think what might have happened if she had not guessed just in time what the French word which had eluded her meant.

Mrs. Belton who walked beside her, was as usual chattering and declaring it was incredible that such a thing could happen.

She reiterated over and over again what everybody already knew, that it must have been a deliberate attempt on the life of the Duke of Wellington, Lord Kiniston and all the other English guests in the Château.

When they reached the French windows which led into the Salon, they entered to find that Willy had already assembled the rest of the party there and was giving them champagne.

Because she felt limp and frightened by what had occurred, Alecia was glad to sit down in a chair, choosing even in her agitation, one as far away as possible from Lady Lillian.

Lady Lillian claimed she was feeling faint and got in consequence a great deal of sympathy and attention from the gentlemen.

The Duke looked around to see if everybody was assembled and the door into the hall was shut before he said:

"I know we all want to hear how Lady Charis was clever enough to save us from what was undoubtedly a deliberate attempt to destroy us."

Because Alecia had foolishly not expected him to call

on her, she started when he said her name, and her first impulse was to refuse to say anything.

Then as if Lord Kiniston understood what she was feeling, he went to the chair in which she was sitting and with surprising gentleness helped her to her feet.

When he had done so he slipped her arm through his and covered her hand where it lay on his evening-coat with his hand.

A little quiver went through her and she felt as if his strength and the warmth of his fingers was very comforting.

Then as she looked up at him enquiringly there was an expression in his eyes which was very different from any way he had looked at her before.

Again she felt herself quiver with a strange sensation which seemed to flicker through her breasts and touch her lips where he had kissed them.

"Do not be frightened," he said quietly, "just tell us all how you knew what was going to happen."

Because his voice was gentle, yet authoritative, Alecia knew she must do what he told her.

Although it was difficult to find the words, she said a little incoherently:

"P . perhaps it would be . . better for me to . . say n . nothing."

She glanced towards Lady Lillian as she spoke, and as if the latter was suddenly aware of the part she had played in this drama she said hastily:

"I am sure Lady Charis is right. 'The least said, the soonest mended', and after all, no one has been hurt."

"Had it not been for Lady Charis's timely warning," the Duke of Wellington replied, "there would be a very different story to tell, and I insist upon knowing how Lady Charis was clever enough to save us."

136

There was a little murmur of agreement when he finished speaking, and as Lord Kiniston's fingers tightened on her hand, Alecia drew in a deep breath.

"It . . started yesterday," she said in a small, childlike voice, "when . . I went into the . . Conservatory."

She went on to explain how she had seen the two workmen and how she had heard one of them say as they left: "All we need now is the *cosmétique*" but she had not understood what the French word meant.

As she thought Lord Kiniston himself must think her very stupid not to have realised what it could mean, she glanced at him apprehensively, but he smiled at her as she continued:

"When . . luncheon was finished . . I came into this room . . then went into the garden . . intending to read . . ."

Her voice faltered as she explained how she heard through the open window the *Duc* asking Lady Lillian to bring the Duke of Wellington and Lord Kiniston into the Conservatory at exactly a quarter to ten, saying he had presents for both of them, and also one for her.

"I have never heard such nonsense!" Lady Lillian cried. "Lady Charis is telling a lot of lies!"

"Kindly allow Lady Charis to continue without interruption," the Duke said sharply.

The way he spoke made it impossible for Lady Lillian to say any more.

Shyly, because she was so embarrassed, Alecia then told how after dinner she had gone up to her room and stood at the window to look out into the garden.

She had seen the two men, who she thought were the same ones she had seen the previous day, go towards the Conservatory carrying something, and then

137

they had been followed by another man whom she felt vaguely resembled the *Duc*.

"My God!" Willy said in a low voice. "The swine only pretended to go to Paris to have an alibi after he had killed us all!"

The Duke gave him a sharp glance, but did not rebuke him, and Alecia finished:

"When I saw the three men leaving the Conservatory, I was certain that the one in the cloak was the *Duc* and yet I was .. stupid enough not to .. suspect what he had .. done until when we reached the Conservatory .. suddenly I guessed what .. *cosmétique* meant."

Her voice died away into silence, and once again she looked up at Lord Kiniston.

"In that moment," he said quietly, "you saved all our lives and, most important of all, the life of the Duke!"

Then as gently as he had raised her he helped her back into the chair in which she had been sitting, and picking up a glass of champagne put it into her hand.

The Duke took over.

"Now listen to me," he said. "I am sure you would want me first of all to thank Lady Charis from the bottom of our hearts for her cleverness in realising the truth and giving the alarm so that we were all saved. Any other woman might have been too shy to suggest that anything so unpredictable was about to happen. But as those of you who are soldiers know, a split second can mean the difference between life and death."

There was a murmur around the room and the Duke said simply:

"I thank you, Lady Charis, on behalf of us all. There are no words in which we can express more eloquently our gratitude."

138

Alecia blushed and looked down as the Duke continued:

"Now I have something very important to say, and that is that I want you all to give me your word of honour that no one will speak outside this room of what occurred here tonight!"

He paused before he went on:

"Lord Kiniston, I am quite certain, will be able to find a plausible explanation of how the over-stoked boiler set the Conservatory on fire, but as far as the rest of us are concerned, we know nothing about it and are not interested."

Everybody looked surprised and the Duke said sternly:

"Most of you are aware of the difficulties, the problems and the discussions there have been about a reduction in the size of the Army of Occupation. If what has happened tonight should be known, I am certain the British Government, who are already apprehensive that if I go to Paris there might be attempts on my life, would change their minds, and the thirty thousand men who are scheduled to go home would be obliged to remain in France."

He paused before he continued in his clear, dry manner:

"That would cause consternation amongst the French who at the moment are very relieved that I am to reduce the number of men who have to be fed and housed at their expense. I am sure you will understand therefore and give me your word of honour that in no circumstances will you discuss this matter, and on no account must you relay it to England in your letters."

"I understand, dear Duke," Marianne Patterson said, "and of course I promise you that I and my sisters will tell no one. We are only so thankful, so very, very thankful, that you are alive and unhurt."

There was a little throb in her voice which Alecia was sure pleased the Duke, for he gave her what was for him a very intimate smile.

"Speaking on behalf of myself and my guests," Lord Kiniston said, "I am certain Your Grace can trust us, and those of us who wear the British uniform take what you have said as an order which will be obeyed."

When the other officers present had made it clear that they agreed with this, Willy, as if he felt that it was a mistake to end the evening on a gloomy note, said in his usual good-humoured manner:

"I think this is the moment when we should drink a toast to British integrity and the downfall of all villains who fancy themselves as a modern Guy Fawkes!"

The way he spoke brought a little titter of laughter from them all, and they had indeed been looking very solemn.

Then as Willy and Colonel Felton-Hervey went around with the champagne filling up the glasses, voices began to rise and soon the whole room was chattering.

Because she felt as if she could not bear any more, Alecia said in a whisper to Lord Kiniston standing beside her:

"Do you think I could .. go to bed?"

"Yes, of course," he answered. "You have been through quite enough for one day, but try to believe it is something I know will not occur again."

He drew her to her feet, and as she put her arm through his he said:

"You can just slip away. I think it would be a mistake for people to start plying you with questions which in the circumstances are inevitable."

140

"Please .. do not let anybody .. notice me," Alecia pleaded.

As they were all talking to anyone who would listen, of what had happened, Lord Kiniston managed to steer Alecia to the door without anyone noticing it.

Then he took her into the hall and as they walked towards the staircase she realised in surprise that there were no footmen on duty.

She was about to say so to Lord Kiniston, when she was aware that he had realised the same thing.

"They were in on the plot!" he exclaimed. "They have run away so that they cannot be interrogated when our bodies are found!"

Alecia gave a little cry of horror and he added:

"They will be back in the morning and, as the Duke has suggested, we will behave as if nothing has happened."

"The fire will not .. burn the rest of the .. Château?" Alecia asked nervously.

"Willy has already anticipated that we might be worried about that," Lord Kiniston said, "and the British sentries on duty have put it out, I am quite certain, most efficiently."

He smiled at her as they reached the bottom of the stairs, then as she put out her hand to say goodnight, he said:

"There is no need for me to tell you that you were utterly and completely magnificent!"

Because it was not what she had expected him to say Alecia blushed.

Then he took her hand in his and raised it to his lips and she felt the pressure of them on the softness of her skin.

She felt a strange sensation like a little flash of lightning running through her before Lord Kiniston repeated:

"Absolutely magnificent, and very lovely!"

For a moment they just looked at each other and it was impossible for Alecia to look away.

Then because she wanted to go on talking to him, but at the same time knew she should leave him, she took her hand from his and ran up the stairs as quickly as she could.

Only as she reached the top did she long to look back at him to see if he was still there.

Then she told herself that he would have gone back to the party, and she would feel disappointed because he had done so.

She therefore went on towards her bedroom without looking back.

She had no idea that Lord Kiniston stood watching her go and remained in the same position for some minutes after she had vanished from sight.

When Alecia awoke in the morning, her first thoughts were of Lord Kiniston. She knew she had gone to bed thinking of him and feeling his lips not only on her hand, but also on her mouth.

It seemed in retrospect incredible that he had actually kissed her when he had lain on top of her on the ground.

Then she told herself that it had meant nothing to him, but was just relief that they were alive and not dead.

She remembered her father telling her once that in some country after an earthquake those who survived it would kiss each other, and even make love, although

142

Alecia was not certain exactly what that entailed, amongst the ruins.

"I can understand how glad they were to be alive, Papa," she had said.

She was sure that was what Lord Kiniston's kiss had meant and nothing more.

But she knew that when the time came for her to return to England in disgrace with his anger doubtless ringing in her ears, it would be something she would always remember.

Sarah brought her breakfast in bed and said it was His Lordship's orders that she was to rest as long as possible.

"None o' them other ladies is awake yet, M'Lady," she added, "but I didn't think as you'd be asleep for long."

She then started to tell Alecia in tones of horror how it had been discovered this morning by the Major Domo when he came on duty that the Conservatory had been burnt down during the night.

"It's fortunate, M'Lady, none of us was burnt to death in our beds!" Sarah said. "An' downstairs, they're sayin' the same thing!"

"I expect they over-stoked the boilers which keep the Conservatory warm for the flowers," Alecia observed carelessly.

"Yer can't trust these Frenchies to do anythin' right!" Sarah remarked scathingly.

Alecia thought that was a typical British attitude towards a foreigner.

Because she had no wish to stay in bed and was regretting that she was unable to ride before breakfast as she had hoped to do with Lord Kiniston, she got up and dressed in one of her prettiest gowns.

She was just having her hair arranged by Sarah when there was a knock on the door and when Sarah opened it a footman stood there who said in French:

"*Monsieur Milord* wishes to see Her Ladyship as soon as she is ready."

Alecia felt her heart leap and looking at her reflection in the mirror she realised that her eyes had lit almost as if they had caught the sunshine.

"I want to see him," she confessed to herself.

She knew it was because he had shown her last night how proud he was of her that she wanted to be with him, to hear him praise her, and perhaps, although she was quite certain it was something that would not happen, he would kiss her again.

"After all, I am .. supposed to be his fiancée," she told herself, "and in the .. circumstances he might be expected to .. kiss me."

Even as she thought of it she told herself it would be a mistake, since she was not Charis, to allow what had been a very formal relationship to become something different.

She was certain that because she had told him she had no wish to marry him he was treating her, as he had suggested, like a friend until they knew each other better.

But because he had kissed her as he covered her body with his to protect her from any injury, she felt as if everything had altered between them, and, although it might be wrong, it was something that could not be undone.

"I want to see him .. and he is .. waiting for me!" she told herself jubilantly.

Springing up from the dressing-table stool she hurried across the room while Sarah was still closing the door.

"I've not finished your hair, M'Lady!" she exclaimed.

"It looks very nice," Alecia said quickly, "and His Lordship wants me."

She did not wait to argue any further but ran down the passage and down the stairs.

Now the footmen were back in the hall and she was sure the Major Domo, who had undoubtedly been in on the plot, was not far away.

She was however not thinking of that as she hurried down the passage to the room where she knew she would find Lord Kiniston.

He was, as she expected, sitting at his desk, and he rose as she entered.

Then as she moved towards him, her eyes on his face, she thought he looked somehow different from the way he had looked before.

There was, she was certain, a glint of admiration in his eyes as he looked at her, and she thought, although she could not be sure, it was something more than admiration.

Then as she dropped him a little curtsy, he said:

"You are all right? You slept well?"

"Very well, thank you, and there has been .. no further .. trouble?"

"None," he answered. "I was informed by the officer on duty last night that a fire was reported in the Conservatory which was dealt with quickly and efficiently and there is no damage except to the Conservatory, which no longer exists."

Alecia gave a little sigh of relief. Then she said:

"Now we can .. forget it, and the others will not .. talk to me .. about it, .. will they?"

"Not if they obey the Duke," Lord Kiniston said. "But I have a question to ask you, Charis, or rather I

145

would be grateful if you could explain to me something I find hard to understand."

"What is that?"

Her thoughts were still on last night, and she was wondering if, because she had been so embarrassed, when she had to relate to them all exactly what had occurred, she had forgotten something important.

Lord Kiniston came from behind his desk and when he reached her side he handed her a letter.

"Will you read this?" he asked.

Alecia took it from him and saw it was a letter written in English, although in a not very educated hand. At the same time, the writing was clear and easy to read.

It began:

"My Lord,

When I saw you last, you mentioned to me that Your Lordship was considering moving your horses from Newmarket to Epsom since to train there would be more convenient when Your Lordship is in London and nearer of course to Kiniston Hall in Buckinghamshire.

I recently received a visit from the Viscount Turnbury, who is very interested in the horses in your stables. When he was here his wife asked me if it might be possible for me to show them over the House.

I hope I did nothing wrong, but I took the Viscountess round and she was exceedingly impressed by the comfort of it and the delightful gardens. His Lordship then asked me if there was any possibility of your selling him the stables, as he had heard rumours in London that it was your intention to do so and at the same time to dispose of the horses.

I could only tell His Lordship that I would write to

146

you, and explain the situation, and he thanked me profusely, saying that he and his wife were on their way to Suffolk and asking me to inform him as quickly as possible if in fact you would consider selling him the whole property, including the contents of the house and any horses Your Lordship may wish to dispose of.

I am therefore writing immediately to ascertain Your Lordship's wishes in the matter, and as the Viscount was so insistent that he required an early reply, to ask Your Lordship's instructions.

It was only as the Viscount was leaving that I realised I had seen his wife before at the Spring Meeting last year. It would be impossible to forget her as she is so beautiful, and she was then Lady Charis Langley.

I hope Your Lordship is in good health, and that you will soon be returning to England, now that the War has come to an end.

> I remain,
> Your Humble and Obedient Servant,
> Frederick Matthews."

As Alecia finished reading the letter she put it down on the desk beside her.

Without looking at Lord Kiniston she clasped her hands together, squeezing her fingers until the knuckles showed white, and finally she said in a very low voice:

"I .. I am .. sorry!"

"Is that all you have to say?" Lord Kiniston enquired.

"I .. I am sorry," Alecia repeated. "I .. I will return to England immediately .. I .. I was only waiting until Charis .. was married."

"So it is true! The wife of young Turnbury is Charis Langley!"

It was impossible to speak and Alecia only nodded.

"Then who, in the name of Heaven, are you?"

"I am her first cousin . . and we are . . considered to be . . very much . . alike."

"So alike," Lord Kiniston said, "that everybody has been deceived by you, although I thought it very strange when you arrived that you were frightened about something and, considering how fêted and acclaimed Lady Charis has been, you seemed unsure of yourself and often shy."

"I . . I have lived very . . quietly in the country . . with my father."

"You have not been to London?"

"N . no."

"And you have never been kissed until I kissed you?"

Now the colour flared in Alecia's cheeks, and feeling she could not bear this interrogation she moved away towards the window to stand looking out blindly into the sunlit garden.

She knew as she did so that the dream-world in which she had been living had come to an end, and now she would have to go home and never see Lord Kiniston again.

Almost as if she was struck by lightning, she knew as she thought of it, that not only had she no wish to leave him, but that she loved him.

It seemed absurd, ridiculous, altogether impossible to feel that way about a man of whom she had been so frightened.

And yet she could feel her whole body throbbing with an inexpressible agony because she must leave him, because undoubtedly he was very angry with her and would at any moment now denounce her as an imposter.

He spoke just behind her, and as she had not heard him approach her she started as he asked:

"What is your real name?"

It was difficult to speak, but somehow she managed to say:

"A . Alecia .. Stambrook."

"And now," Lord Kiniston said, "having involved us both in this extremely complicated situation, will you tell me how we are to get out of it?"

"I .. I will .. go away .. at once," Alecia said. "I .. expected to have to .. do that."

"You will go back to England?"

"Yes .. to Papa .. we live in Little Langley .. which is the village adjoining what was .. Charis's home."

"Who, when I sent for her, asked you to come in her place because she wished to marry?"

"Y.yes .. she was very much in love with the Viscount .. and she thought .. you would .. forbid her to be married because his mother .. had died only just .. a few weeks previously."

Alecia drew in her breath before she went on:

"I beg of you not to be angry with her .. they love each other so .. ideally and completely .. just as Mama loved Papa .. that she could not leave him .. and do what you wanted."

"She might have been honest with me and told me the truth."

"She thought of that .. but she was certain .. because we both expected you to be very .. old that you would not understand .. and would insist on her waiting conventionally for perhaps .. a year before you would allow her to be .. married."

"It certainly seems an extraordinarily heartless action on the bride-groom's part," Lord Kiniston said dryly.

149

"That is what they were .. afraid you would .. say," Alecia said, "but now they are married .. and you can do .. nothing about it."

"I must accept that," Lord Kiniston replied. "But there still remains the problem of you. I want you to tell me why you acquiesced in acting a lie, which seems somehow alien to your nature."

"I .. I think Mama .. too would have been shocked," Alecia said, "except that she knew that .. love is more important than anything else .. and Charis is very, very much .. in love with Viscount Turnbury."

There was a little note of wistfulness in Alecia's voice as she knew that she too was in love, but as far as she was concerned it was hopeless, and the only thing she could do was to hurry home to England as quickly as possible.

"And because you are fond of your cousin, you agreed, without any inducement to her suggestion that you should impersonate her and deceive me."

The note of condemnation in Lord Kiniston's voice cut through Alecia like a knife.

"It .. it was not only that I .. wanted to help Charis but .. also Papa."

"In what way?" Lord Kiniston asked sharply.

Alecia drew in her breath.

She wished she did not have to explain things to him, but she knew that not only was he entitled to an explanation, but that somehow it was impossible not to answer his questions.

"Charis's father was my mother's brother," she said in a low voice, "and when he died, just two months after my mother's death, we no longer received the regular supplies of food from the estate on which we depended. Papa writes books but they make very little money and I was really .. desperate because the tradespeople would no longer give us credit .. then Charis came to see me."

"So she paid you for doing what she wanted!"

Alecia shut her eyes.

It seemed sordid and humiliating, and yet now she had to be honest.

"She .. gave me .. £500," she faltered, "which will keep Papa .. well and properly fed for a .. long time."

"I presume she also provided you with the clothes you are wearing."

"A lot of them are hers," Alecia agreed, "because she was having a new trousseau. We have always been able to wear each other's things .. and mine were in .. rags."

She bent her head as she spoke, feeling that Lord Kiniston had driven her down into the dust and if she was kneeling at his feet she could not go any lower.

"Let me go .. home at .. once!" she pleaded. "I know you do not .. understand, and I am very .. ashamed of the way I have .. deceived you. Although I have been terrified in case you should .. find me out, I will never .. never forget that I have been here .. and that I have .. met you."

"You will never forget me?" Lord Kiniston enquired.

Alecia did not speak and after a moment he asked:

"Why will you never forget me?"

Again there was silence and he said:

"Look at me, Alecia! I want you to tell me the truth – the real truth as to why you will not forget me!"

Because it was impossible not to obey him, very slowly Alecia turned towards him and raised her face to his.

He saw the fear in her eyes, and yet he would have

151

been very obtuse if he had not realised there was another expression in them too.

"Tell me," he asked softly, "why you will not forget me."

For a moment she just stared at him and he knew her whole body was trembling before he said:

"You have told me you have never been kissed except by me. I thought that was so when I kissed you after the explosion, but I want to make certain I was not mistaken, and that your lips are as sweet and innocent as they seemed then."

He put his arms around her and drew her against him.

Before Alecia could take her eyes from his or realise what was happening, his lips were on hers.

Because he knew how inexperienced and innocent she was, at first it was a very gentle, tender kiss. Until as he felt her lips respond he became more possessive, more demanding, as he drew her closer and closer to him.

It was then that the love Alecia felt for him rose like a wave through her body and ran like sunshine from her breasts, into her throat and from her throat to her lips.

It was a sensation she had never known and never imagined, and it was so ecstatic, so utterly and completely rapturous, that she knew this was what she had always wanted.

It was in the music she heard when she was alone in the woods, in the beauty which had aroused her but which had always seemed a little distant, because she was alone.

It was love, the love that her mother and father had

known, and Charis had found with Harry Turnbury, and which she had prayed might one day come to her.

"I love him!" she wanted to cry aloud, but there was no need for words.

Her body quivered against Lord Kiniston's and as he kissed her she gave him her heart and soul and was no longer herself, but his.

Only when Alecia felt as if they had reached Heaven and she was no longer on earth did he raise his head and asked:

"Is that what you expected from a kiss?"

"I . . I love you!" Alecia whispered. "I love you . . and before you send me away . . please . . kiss me again!"

"You really think I could let you go?"

Then he was kissing her, fiercely, demandingly, as if he was afraid of losing her.

She felt the fire on his lips and it lit a little flame within herself so that she wanted only that he should go on kissing her and she should never again have to face the world outside or to be parted from him.

Only when Lord Kiniston finally raised his head to look down at her did she, with an inarticulate little murmur, hide her face against his shoulder.

"How can I have been so blind," he asked, "as to be deceived into thinking that you could be the young woman whose name has been bandied about in the Clubs of St. James's and who figures in the Betting-Book at White's?"

"F.forgive me," Alecia pleaded.

"How can I do anything else?" Lord Kiniston asked. "After all, if you had been here last night, I would not now be here to see you and to kiss you!"

Alecia made an exclamation before she asked:

"Suppose he . . tries . . again?"

"I doubt if he will do that," Lord Kiniston said.

"Why . . not?"

"Because unless I am a very bad judge of character, he will know that he has failed, and will expect to be arrested, which is something that he will make sure does not happen. In fact, he will simply disappear, and I doubt if we will hear from the *Duc* de St. Briere until his Château is empty and ready for his return."

Alecia gave a deep sigh and asked:

"And you are . . sure you are . . safe?"

"You sound as if you really mind whether I am or not," Lord Kiniston said.

"Of course I mind!" Alecia protested.

"In which case I am afraid you will have to continue to look after me and make sure that I get into no more trouble of that sort."

He saw Alecia stare and said:

"The only way we can extricate ourselves honourably from the situation you and Charis contrived between you is for you to marry me."

"M.marry you?"

Her voice was indistinct, but her eyes shone so brightly that Lord Kiniston felt dazzled by them. Before he could speak she turned her head to the side to ask:

"But of course . . we will have to wait for the . . six months that you said was . . essential so that we can get to . . know each other and find out whether or not we are . . compatible!"

Lord Kiniston laughed, and it was a very happy sound.

"I have no intention of waiting six months," he said. "What we are going to do, my darling, is much more simple than that. We are going back to England immediately on urgent family business, and the moment we reach Kiniston Hall we will be married quietly by my private Chaplain."

Alecia gave a little cry of joy as he went on:

"Then when we have time, we will talk to your cousin Charis and Harry Turnbury and decide when we will announce their marriage and ours, and leave the gossip-writers to sort out, as undoubtedly they will, what has happened."

"It sounds too .. wonderful to be .. true!" Alecia gasped. "But you are quite .. sure .. ?"

"Quite, quite sure," Lord Kiniston smiled. "I want you as I have never wanted any woman before in my life, and I have no intention of losing you."

"It .. cannot be .. true! I thought every moment I was with .. you would be my last .. and I would only have that to .. remember when I went .. home in disgrace."

She could not help her voice breaking and tears filled her eyes.

"You will never leave me for a moment."

Then he was kissing away her tears, and her lips, until she smiled again from sheer happiness.

After what seemed a fleeting moment of glory and a rapture that could only be divine, Lord Kiniston said:

"Now we have to get busy, my lovely one. I am going to see the Duke of Wellington to explain to him that I have to leave for England as quickly as possible. What you have to do is to pack your boxes and be ready at the very latest in an hour's time."

"In an hour's time?" Alecia enquired. "But .. how can we do that?"

"It is only a question of organisation," he replied.

"There are enough servants in the house to pack your boxes, and all I have to do is to set the wheels in motion."

He looked down at her face which was so radiant with happiness that he thought no woman could look more lovely and added:

"I think when we get to England, we will allow your Cousin Charis to have the £20,000 she wants, and we will also permit them to buy my house and my stables at Newmarket, but not all the horses. I will keep the best for you."

"I want to ride with you . . I want to be with you . . I want to do everything with you . . " Alecia said passionately.

"But of course," Lord Kiniston agreed, "but most of all, my darling, you have to look after me and save me not only from being blown up by bombs, but also from tiresome, possessive women!"

He thought as he spoke how very lucky he was to have escaped both from Lady Lillian and from the Duke's match-making.

He knew, although Alecia would not understand, that because he loved her so completely she would save him in the future from a great many embarrassments that he had not been able to avoid in the past.

"I love her!" he told himself, "and I want nothing more than to be her husband and to look after her."

Lady Kiniston waited in the huge State Bedroom at Kiniston Hall.

She looked very small and ethereal in the satin-draped bed with its canopy of gilt cupids carrying garlands of roses.

She had been married early in the evening in the

Chapel, fragrant with the scent of flowers, exactly three hours after she had seen her future home for the first time.

She had found the journey long, irksome, and of course frightening on her way to Cambrai.

It was very different when she travelled with Lord Kiniston with horses that seemed to fly along the roads as if each was a winged Pegasus.

Every moment she had sat beside him, every word he said to her, every time he touched her hand, she thought she fell more hopelessly and overwhelmingly in love with the most wonderful man she had ever met in the whole of her life.

"You are not tired, my darling?" he had asked when they reached Dover in his private yacht which had been waiting for them at Calais.

"I slept peacefully," Alecia replied, "and I thought the waves were enveloping me like your arms, and I was safe and so were you."

"Tonight it will not be the waves that hold you in their arms," Lord Kiniston replied.

Alecia's eyes widened.

"You mean . . ?"

"I have sent instructions ahead," he replied, "and we will be married as soon as we arrive at my home."

He knew Alecia was surprised and he explained:

"It is unconventional, my precious one, for you to be travelling without a chaperon, but I hope since we left with such speed and no one except the Duke was aware that we were going, we shall not be gossiped about."

He kissed her hand before he continued:

"But in my home you must have a chaperon, and who better than your husband?"

157

"Oh .. Drogo .. I cannot believe this is .. true and that you really .. love me."

"I will convince you of that tonight!"

When she blushed he smiled and added:

"I adore you, I love your innocence and the fact that no one has ever taught you about love except me."

"How could you think I would want them to?" Alecia asked.

Because it was difficult to explain to her why she was so different from other women, he could only kiss her lips.

There was a well-sprung, light travelling-chariot waiting for them at Dover, and Lord Kiniston's own horses were waiting to take over every fifteen miles until they reached Kiniston Hall.

They stopped for Luncheon at an old village Posting Inn where there were no guests except themselves, and the food and wine which was provided for them by Lord Kiniston's Chef was delicious.

But Alecia could only think of how much she loved the man beside her, and how wildly and ecstatically happy she was every time he looked at her.

"How could I have .. dreamed or .. guessed all this would .. happen to .. me?" she said.

"I think you must have had a Guardian Angel looking after you," Lord Kiniston smiled.

" .. and you," Alecia said softly.

"I am sure your prayers did that."

As Lord Kiniston spoke he thought he had never known a woman who prayed, as his Mother had, and one who was what he wanted as his wife and the mother of his children.

When they reached Kiniston Hall he insisted that Alecia went immediately to her room to rest.

"It has been a long journey, whatever you may say, my precious," he said, "and I want you to look beautiful for me tonight because I think that both of us will always remember our wedding-day."

"How could I forget it?" Alecia asked.

Alecia knelt beside Lord Kiniston in the ancient and very beautiful Chapel in front of his Chaplain, who had loved him ever since he had been a small boy.

Lord Kiniston thought it was the most moving moment of his life.

The Chaplain blessed them with a sincerity which brought tears to Alecia's eyes, and she was sure he spoke for God.

Afterwards there was a glass of champagne for everybody in the household who were the only people to know they had been married and they had promised Lord Kiniston to keep the wedding secret.

Then he sent Alecia up to bed and Sarah undressed her saying as she did so:

"You look so lovely, M'Lady! I feels as if you was an angel come down from Heaven to dwell amongst us."

"I hope you will always feel like that, Sarah," Alecia smiled.

When she got into bed and was alone she prayed that she might make her husband happy and not disappoint him.

He came into the room and when he saw her in the great bed he thought no one could look more lovely and at the same time so spiritual yet utterly and completely desirable.

He sat down facing her and said:

"If you are feeling too tired, darling, after our journey,

then although it will be hard to leave you, I will let you rest tonight."

"How could you think of anything so . . cruel or so unkind?" Alecia asked. "I want to be . . close to you I want to be . . sure you love me . . and I would be . . frightened all alone in this big bed!"

Lord Kiniston gave her a smile of sheer happiness.

He took off his robe and got into the bed beside her, and holding her close to him said:

"I will never allow you to be frightened again!"

"Suppose there are still . . Frenchmen trying to . . kill you?"

"How could they succeed if you are with me? And while we are on our honeymoon we must forget the French, and think only of ourselves."

Alecia moved a little closer to him to whisper:

"Suppose I . . disappoint you . . and you wish instead you had married . . Lady Lillian?"

Lord Kiniston turned her face up to his.

"Who is Lady Lillian?" he asked. "Are there any other women in the world? I can think of only one and she is so perfect, so adorable, so ideal in every possible way that I love her as I have never loved anyone before or will in the future."

Alecia gave a little sigh.

"That is a beautiful thing to say to me, and I have . . prayed and . . prayed that I will make you . . happy."

"I am happy now," Lord Kiniston replied, "and I wonder why I ever thought I was happy in the past. What have you done to me, Alecia, that the whole world has changed since I met you?"

He pushed back the hair from her forehead as he said:

"It is not because you are the most beautiful person

alive, it is not because I adore your character, your personality, your innocence and your purity. It is because you are utterly and completely what I thought I would never find in any woman."

"Oh, darling, you are making me frightened," Alecia protested. "Suppose you find I am not as perfect as you think I am?"

"I know you are!" Lord Kiniston insisted. "And when you prayed in the Chapel you would make me happy, I was thanking God that I had been so fortunate as to find the counterpart of myself – the woman who I firmly believe was meant for me since the beginning of time."

He kissed her forehead before he went on:

"You are all the things I am not, and therefore together we make one complete person and because our love will protect us and keep us safe, nothing wrong or evil shall touch us."

He was saying what Alecia had always longed to hear from the man who loved her!

She was so moved that she put out her arm and pulled Lord Kiniston's head down to hers.

"Kiss me," she said. "Please . . kiss me. Teach me to love you . . as you . . want to be loved . . I am so very, very . . grateful that we are . . together."

"We are together," Lord Kiniston agreed, "and no one shall ever separate us."

Then he was kissing her, kissing her passionately, and at the same time with a tenderness that had something reverent in it.

He knew, because she was so young and so innocent that he must be very gentle.

At the same time, as he kissed her he realised the fire within him was lighting an answering flame within

Alecia, and that, as he had said, his love would make them one complete person.

Then as the flames increased and became the Divine Light which is the light of God, Lord Kiniston carried Alecia up into a special Heaven where there is no evil.

Only the perfection and the purity of the true love which casts out fear.